IT WAS
SHOWDOWN TIME...

"Whatcha doin' in Salt Creek, Slocum?"

"Lookin' for a bunch of buzzards who shot some friends."

"Lost some friends, did yuh?" Bullets looked grim. "I lost a couple, too. A bad shootout."

Slocum shifted his position. "What's your handle?"

"They call me Bullethead."

Slocum nodded. "Funny thing. This polecat said that someone called 'Bullethead' would pay his death off in blood. Just before he died."

Bullets swallowed hard. He wanted nothing in the world more than to kill this hombre. But there was no way he could outdraw Slocum. It'd be instant death. Bullets would just reach over easy and shoot the bastard with the derringer he had in his sleeve. He'd never expect that.

"I figger you're trying to push me."

"You shot two men in Tucson. You shot at me. Your bunch bushwhacked five of my friends." Slocum's eyes glittered hard. "Your time is up."

OTHER BOOKS BY JAKE LOGAN

JAKE LOGAN

SLOCUM AND THE GUNFIGHTER'S RETURN

B

BERKLEY BOOKS, NEW YORK

SLOCUM AND THE GUNFIGHTER'S RETURN

A Berkley Book / published by arrangement with
the author

PRINTING HISTORY
Berkley edition / December 1988

ISBN: 0-425-11265-9

A BERKLEY BOOK ® TM 757,375
Berkley Books are published by The Berkley Publishing Group,
200 Madison Avenue, New York, N.Y. 10016.
The name "BERKLEY" and the "B" logo
are trademarks belonging to Berkley Publishing Corporation.

PRINTED IN THE UNITED STATES OF AMERICA.

10 9 8 7 6 5 4 3 2 1

1

The sun was a scalding yellow eye in the sky, and it hit like hammer blows on Slocum, riding the high canyon trail. Everything nearby was seared stone and scorched brittlebush, and not till he passed the towering wall of stone that blocked his view did he get a breeze and see the gorge below.

What he saw made the green eyes in his rugged face glitter like ice. A girl, her blond hair shimmering in the sun, and her cowboy escort were riding a narrow trail. And waiting just ahead, crouched behind a huge boulder, were two gunmen, one bearded, the other bulky, both holding pistols. An ambush.

There was no way for Slocum to get down to the

gorge without miles of riding; he swung off the roan and pulled his Sharps rifle.

The gunmen sprang out, pistols pointing, forcing the riders to pull up. The bearded gunman spoke harshly to the cowboy, who dismounted slowly. Slocum watched, his face hard. Angry words floated up to Slocum.

Suddenly the bearded gunman fired. The cowboy fell back, twisted in agony, and lay still. The gunmen turned to the girl, who, after a moment of shock, pulled her gun. It was shot from her hand. She struck her stallion, a powerful black beauty, and he leaped forward. The gunmen coolly watched, smiling, then the bulky man fired. The big stallion stumbled and collapsed. The girl sprang from the saddle, staring in horror at her wounded horse. The men walked toward her. She started to run. They caught her, flung her to the ground; she fought fiercely, and they tumbled about until one punched her, holding her down.

Slocum, who until now had no clear shot, sighted the Sharps and touched the trigger twice. The crack of the rifle echoed in the gorge. As the bullets ripped into them, both gunmen catapulted down, faces to the ground. They lay motionless, blood pouring from their wounds.

There was silence in the gorge.

The sudden violence seemed to have jolted the girl, and she lay petrified, as if she expected her body to get the next blast. She didn't know who had done the shooting—maybe it was Apaches.

Finally she looked up and saw the big, lean man in the blue shirt and Stetson. He stood easy, graceful and strong, on the side wall of the canyon, and she could see no way for him to get down. She got to her feet slowly and looked at her stallion, who was wounded and suffering. She picked up the gun lying near the bearded dead man, looked long and tearfully at the stallion, who was breathing painfully, then fired a bullet into his brain.

She stood still for a long moment.

Slocum watched her. Gutsy girl, he thought. He slid his rifle back into its saddle holster and rested his hand on the the roan's haunches. The girl stood alone, near a huge boulder, looking up.

He couldn't get down to help bury her cowboy; she'd have to do it. He raised his hand in a farewell.

She waved too.

Slocum felt moved as he swung up onto the roan and picked his way over the narrow trail. He wondered if he'd see her again. He could see her standing alone until a climbing wall of stone shut out his view of the gorge.

The rickety houses in the town of Lawson baked under the Arizona sun when Slocum walked the roan down Main Street. Dust lifted off the street with each step of the roan's hooves. It was plenty dry, and Slocum had a thirst to quench at the saloon, but first he stopped at Miller's Livery.

Miller, a bullet-headed smith with powerful arms, looked at the roan with admiration. "Fine animal," he said.

Slocum warmed to Miller instantly as a man with an appreciation of horseflesh.

"Heart of gold, Miller." Slocum looked at the horse's great chest and sturdy legs—legs that many a time had run him out of trouble. He looked at the big dark expressive eyes and the white spot on his forehead, as if from birth he'd been marked to be a star.

"Runs like a streak, too," Miller said, working his hand on the muscular haunches.

"He's the best. I'm Slocum. Grain and curry him." He tossed a coin, which Miller caught deftly.

Looking down the street toward the saloon, Slocum saw a bunch of horses tied to the railing. "What's happening in Lawson, Miller?"

Miller grinned. "This is a nice town, Slocum. But a bad bunch is in from Tombstone. Guzzlin' and kickin' up a fuss. A coupla gunfights for just nothin'. I'd sure steer clear of the saloon."

Slocum shrugged. As far as he could tell, there was always a bad bunch somewhere in the territory. They sprang up like bad weeds. "Got some dust in my throat. Reckon a whiskey or two could clean it."

Miller studied the lean, rugged, green-eyed man in the hard-worn Levi's. "Reckon a man like you goes where he wants to." He rubbed the roan's back. "There's good chow at Aunt Bessie's."

Slocum nodded and walked down the hot dusty street lined with ramshackle huts until he reached the two-story saloon, out of which spewed whiskey voices. The batwing doors creaked when he pushed them open. There was a lot of tobacco smoke, men drinking at the bar, men playing at the card tables, and a few women in tight, flouncy dresses.

He ordered whiskey from a round-faced bartender whose dark hair was parted in the middle and plastered down. He gave Slocum a friendly, inquisitive glance as he slapped down a bottle and a glass.

Slocum drank his whiskey and glanced about. The men collected around the card tables looked a sleazy bunch, wearing hard-worn duds, their faces scarred from gun and knife fights.

They scarcely looked at him, absorbed in the poker game. The players were also mangy except for one clean cowboy with a roughly handsome face and alert brown eyes. Surprisingly, most of the money was piled in front of him, which might explain his easy smile. Slocum also noted a stubble-bearded player, wearing a flat black hat; he had black eyes and a satanic smile that seemed stuck to his lips.

Someone called him Jess, and every so often Jess would needle the winning young cowboy, whose name seemed to be Dustin. But Dustin didn't fluster, he just smiled.

Slocum sensed trouble for the young cowboy and felt sorry for him. He was making the mistake of winning from a gang of cutthroats.

Then Slocum's gaze fixed on the woman talking to one of the men who looked like he belonged to that scurvy bunch. She had good breasts and buttocks, the way he liked them, and a pretty face and creamy skin still unmarked by time and booze.

Though the polecat was talking to her, she didn't appear to be paying much attention, the gaze of her blue eyes wandering over the room. They clicked in place when they hit Slocum. She must have liked what she saw, because, without a word to the passionate polecat, she stood up and started toward him.

Her abrupt move startled Slocum, who glanced at the polecat. His sodden face twisted with anger as he watched her sidle up alongside him.

"Just blow into town?" she asked.

He nodded. Close up, she was even sexier in her gleaming dress, which was cut low to show the top of her bountiful breasts.

She smiled broadly, as if aware that her merchandise

was selling itself and all she had to do was talk. "Looks like you've had a hard time out there."

"Yeah? How can you tell?"

She came closer, her full lips in a seductive smile. "I can always tell when a man's had a hard time." Then she added, "Or wants to. My name is Maude."

"I'm Slocum."

Just then the polecat stomped up, his face dark with anger; he had overheard the name, and now he used it. "Hey, Slocum." He showed yellow teeth in a vicious smile. "Are you fixin' on a short life?"

Slocum turned with a small smile. The man's eyes were glazed a bit with booze, and he was furious because Maude had ignored him for what she thought was a better customer.

Slocum glanced at Maude. She shrugged. It wasn't the first time that men were ready to spill blood because of lust.

"Luke," she said, "be good. Don't make trouble."

"Shut up, you bitch. You walked away from me. To this no-account drifter."

The men at the card table nearby glanced at them— even Jess, the one with the satanic smile. He just shrugged and looked back at his cards, fascinated more by the game.

Slocum, who felt a bit weary from his riding, and cared only about a whiskey, a bit of fun, then a bed to sleep in, preferred to avoid trouble. "Luke," he said gently. "Why don't you go back to your table and have a couple drinks on me? Let's have a peaceful evenin'."

Luke, who felt roughed up by Maude, was having none of it. He interpreted Slocum's peace offer as weakness. And he was going to prove to Maude that she had picked a dud, that he was the better man.

"Mister, I don't want your drinks. I just want you to stand away from that bar, 'cause I'm gonna put you flat out." He stood squarely, with his legs spread out, two big fists cocked, and a vicious snarl on his face.

Slocum shook his head. "Hey, Luke, is there no way to get you to sit down and keep the peace?"

The drinkers at the bar were looking amused, expecting fun of some kind.

Then Luke, determined to put a dramatic stop to any appeal for peace, suddenly swung his right at Slocum's chin.

He was shocked when Slocum brought up his left in a solid block.

Frustrated, Luke threw his left, which also was firmly blocked. Luke showed his teeth, hissed, and swung his fists violently twice; again Slocum put out an iron block.

It was comic, and the drinkers broke into raucous laughter.

Luke, in a fury, yelled, "Fight, you yellow dog."

At that, Slocum swung his right, and his fist, with the muscled power of his back behind it, hit Luke like a thunderbolt. He went down with a thud onto the floor, his eyes rolling up in his head, then going shut.

He lay there in a moment of heavy silence.

Suddenly three men standing around Jess's card game came toward Slocum.

"Wish you hadn't done that, mister." The speaker was a cool-voiced, steely-eyed, sinewy man in a short black hat. He looked to be a fast gunslinger.

Maude spoke up. "Luke was asking for it, Jim. This man didn't want any part of him."

"That's right, Jim," said a cool voice from the table.

It was Jess. "Luke was playing the drunken fool. Let the man be, Jim."

Jim's eyes narrowed, but he said nothing further to Slocum, just bent to pick Luke up off the floor.

Maude quickly jerked at Slocum's sleeve and then started toward the stairs. Slocum glanced coolly at the faces watching him, and they turned away, some faces smiling, others cold.

He sauntered toward the stairs, following Maude.

The room had a crude wooden chest, a chair, and a low bed. Slocum shut the door and turned. Her back was to him, and, wasting no time, she lifted her dress, dropped it, and stood nude. He admired the fine shape of her back, the slender waist widening to fine buttocks, her strong silky thighs and legs. He moved behind her and put his hands over her breasts; they were plump and silky, and the nipples were hard. He stroked her, felt the curves of her, then turned her. She looked like a sex pistol.

She smiled. "You might get your clothes off."

He grunted and peeled off his clothes.

She looked at his excitement and reached for it. "Fine specimen of manhood," she said.

He laughed and pulled her tight against him. "Nothing wrong with you, either."

He felt the velvet of her skin. They moved to the bed, where her full lips made love to him and he saw stars. He slipped over her, his flesh seethed, and his hands slipped behind her buttocks. They moved in rhythm, and he felt her body stiffen with its pleasure. It happened twice, then he felt himself climbing to a pitch, her body moving against his with a strong rhythm until he went off with a shudder.

Afterward, when he had dressed and she still lay on the bed, she said, "You're a fine lover, Slocum."

"Takes one to make one." He grinned, put money on the chest, and went out to the hall.

He went down the stairs carefully, his eyes alert to spot trouble, but no one paid attention. Everyone watched the game where Dustin and Jess were betting a big pot. Slocum quietly drifted over and stood near the bunch.

Jess, with his peculiar smile, asked for one card, Dustin for two. Jess didn't look at his cards and spoke casually. "Where'd you say you rode in from, Dustin? Looks like you been hard travelin'."

"Red River, Jess," Dustin said. "Where men are men."

"And even the women grow beards," said a beady-eyed, hulking man in a crazy gray hat. The bunch stomped their boots and laughed crudely.

Dustin didn't bite. "We got our share o' pretty ladies in Red River."

"Hope they don't play cards like you," said Jim, the man who had helped Luke up, his voice edged with meaning.

Jess glanced at the speaker, amused. "That's Jim Hardy." As if it was enough. The steely-eyed gunman didn't smile.

Slocum's mouth tightened. They were needling young Dustin, but he wasn't taking the bait. He had a stack of money in front of him and didn't care to put it at risk. They sure had young Dustin on the rack. Didn't like him taking out the money. Then Slocum eyed Jim Hardy. Slocum had shot a gambler named Red Hardy three weeks ago in Dodge. The man had been drunk, had bumped him, insulted him, then pulled his gun.

Slocum had been forced to shoot. He wondered if this Jim was kin.

Dustin glanced at his cards and bet forty dollars.

Jess raised him forty. His satanic smile seemed pasted to his face. Dustin didn't smile, just glanced at the evil-eyed bunch watching him, studied his cards, studied Jess, then raised another forty. The pot was big.

Slocum looked again at Jess. He was a gray-eyed man with a stubble-bearded face, a strong jaw, and that strange smile. He had a powerful body, and the Colt in his holster looked worn. It looked like he was the head man of the bunch, who were all scuffed and scarred from lives spent in fighting, thieving, rustling, and God knew what else.

"Figger you got me beat, Dustin? But you ain't." He glanced at Jim Hardy, the fast gunman.

"You ain't coming out of this pot, Dustin," Jess went on, and grinning, he laid out his cards. "Two pairs— aces and queens."

"Reckon you're dead wrong, Jess." Dustin laid out his cards. "Three deuces."

It hit Jess, and for once the satanic smile came off his face. He had lost his poise. Slocum watched his eyes flicker at Jim Hardy.

Dustin reached for the pile.

"Don't anyone touch the money," Jim said, grim-faced, his voice cool. Curiously, he didn't pull his gun, as if the threat of it was enough to stop anyone.

And, to Slocum's amazement, it did. Everyone stood petrified. Dustin froze.

Jim spoke slowly. "Don't know how you got the cards, mister, but don't touch the money."

Again the silence. Then Jim pointed to a scar-faced

man standing next to Dustin. "Willie, pick up the money."

"Hold it." Dustin pushed back his chair, standing. There was a deathlike silence in the saloon. "Is that the way you win, Jess? If your cards don't get it, your boys pick it up?"

Jess laughed. "Don't blame me, Dustin. I'm not taking the money. Jim Hardy is."

"Jim Hardy is your man."

Jess shook his head. "I wouldn't say that. Jim Hardy is his own man."

Jim Hardy's eyes were like blue steel. "If you don't like it, Dustin, you can settle it. Just pull your gun."

The tension crackled as the men in the saloon looked on. Dustin fought his impulse to draw, which meant certain death against this deadly gunslinger.

Then Slocum, standing behind the gunman and not liking what was happening, spoke. "Won't be necessary for Jim Hardy to pull his gun or anyone else," he said.

Everyone turned to look at Slocum. His gun was out, and his eyes were icy. "The cowboy here won fair and square. He gets the money."

Jim Hardy started to turn.

"Hold it." Slocum's tone was cold. He reached to Hardy's holster, pulled his gun, and stuck it in his belt. A grubby man with a thick mustache in the back sneaked his pistol out. Slocum's gun cracked and the man yelled and grabbed at his bloody hand as his gun dropped.

"Don't anybody else be foolish." He turned to Dustin. "Take the money you rightfully won. I'm sure that Jess here wants you to have it. Right, Jess?"

The satanic smile was back on Jess's face. "Sure.

The kid won fair and square. What'd you say your name was, mister?"

"Slocum."

Jim Hardy's steel-blue eyes glittered, as if the name hit him.

Jess glanced at him. "Sure. Only thing, Slocum, I think you insulted Jim Hardy, and he's not one to forget. So what you oughta do is make fast tracks. But Dustin, you stick around. I'm sure you want to give me a game to get my money back."

Dustin grinned. "You'll get your chance, Jess. Sometime soon. But I reckon I'll go off with my friend Slocum for now. Like to count my winnings."

Jess looked hard but said nothing.

They backed out of the saloon, Slocum holding his gun on them. "Don't come out," he warned.

Outside, they went for the horses at the railing. Slocum, keeping an eye on the saloon doors, grabbed a buckskin, untied the other horses, and fired, sending them galloping nervously up the street.

Slocum, in front of Dustin, raced to the livery. The roan was at the railing. He jumped off the saddle of the buckskin and went for the roan. He had just reached it when the door of the livery pushed open and Luke appeared with his gun, grinning.

"Well, mister, I been waitin' for you."

Slocum stared at him. Luke wasn't aware yet of what had happened in the saloon.

"What the hell do you want, Luke? You lost that fight fair and square. We win a few, lose a few. That's life."

Luke rubbed his bruised cheekbone, still keeping his gun pointed at Slocum. "I reckon you can hit better than me, mister. But can you pull your gun better?"

Slocum frowned. "You look plenty fast now that you have your gun out."

Luke gritted his teeth. "You don't think I'm gonna shoot you down in cold blood? I ain't that kind. I'm goin' to give you a draw. Just didn't want you ridin' off." Keeping his eyes fixed on Slocum, he slowly put his gun back in its holster.

"Luke," Slocum said calmly, "you're a good fella. Step aside. I've got nothin' against you."

"But I got plenty 'gainst you. You made me look like a mangy mutt. And you're gonna pay." He sneered. "You may be able to punch, but let's see if you've got nerve with a gun."

There was a dim shout at the other end of town as a man came out of the saloon to find the horses scattered. Though Luke was curious, he didn't take his eyes from Slocum.

"Hey, Luke," said Dustin. "Be smart. Let us ride. You won't be sorry."

"Stay outa this, kid, and figger yourself lucky," the man growled.

Slocum's jaw hardened. "Afraid we're running out of time. I ask you again, like a good fella, step aside and nobody gets hurt."

Luke snarled, "You don't understand, mister. I *want* someone to get hurt. *You.* Now pull your gun or I'll shoot you down like a dog."

Other shouts came from down the street.

Slocum shook his head and watched Luke's yellow eyes glisten and his hand start for his holster.

But the sound of only one gun barked, and Luke dropped his gun, grabbed his shooting arm, and with an amazed face stared at the blood gushing.

Dustin yelled from his saddle. "Hey, Luke, some men have more luck than brains."

Slocum slipped his gun into its holster and jumped into the saddle. When he looked back, he could see men from the saloon trying to grab their scattered horses.

2

Slocum's roan ached to run, and he let it go, pleasuring in the stretch of the powerful legs as they drummed the earth. But Dustin's mare couldn't stick, so Slocum had to tighten the reins.

They rode a trail that ran roughly parallel to the canyon and then swung west until they reached a crested ridge. Slocum stopped to look back. Five riders, small in the distance, were cutting their trail. A mean bunch, out for a quick hanging and easy money.

Dustin pulled a bottle of whiskey from his saddlebag and offered it to Slocum, who took a swig.

"Can't thank you enough, Slocum. You sure saved my hide."

Slocum wiped his lips. He liked Dustin, a gutsy

cowboy who wouldn't let himself be pushed. "Didn't like the setup against you."

"Thing I hated was Jess stacking me against Jim Hardy."

"Who is Hardy?"

"A deadly gunslinger. A real killer. He's got a big rep. They say he's fast as Doc Holliday. Used to ride with Ringo, I heard."

Slocum smiled. Funny about gunmen with big reps. Doc Holliday was a fabled gunslinger, yet he happened to know that sometimes he couldn't hit the side of a barn. He'd shoot cockeyed wild. Men like Hickok and Holliday and James all gloried in big reps and notched their killings, as if it made them bigger men. But Slocum had met quiet gunmen who bothered nobody, but, when crossed, they did the kind of shooting that could make them legends.

Dustin took a drink. "I saw Hardy in action against a tough Texan who said the wrong thing. Hardy stared, then told him to pull his gun. The Texan did, and it seemed to me that Hardy watched his move, then made his own. A streak o' lightning."

Slocum's face was grim. "Wonder if he's kin to Red Hardy who I ran into in Dodge. A gambler."

"Wouldn't know. What happened?"

"Bumped me, then called me a clumsy drunk. I didn't like it and advised him he'd live a lot longer if he was more polite. He cussed me, told me my time was up, and went for his gun."

"What happened?"

"Well, I'm here to tell about it. More men are wiped out by whiskey, Dustin, than by women." Then Slocum smiled. "You looked ready to face Jim Hardy."

"I was shakin'."

"Took guts. I liked that." Slocum stared back at the riders. They were still coming, a bit bigger on the horizon. "Tell me, why did they rile you like that? Just because you had their money? Bad losers?"

Dustin shook his head. "Couldn't figure it. Not the first time I won a big pot, but never ran into such a stink about it."

Slocum looked back at the riders. They were racing hard but still far away. "Reckon Jess hates to lose."

Dustin looked thoughtful. "He sure wanted my hide. Why'd he want it? That's the puzzle. Seemed like it didn't matter if I won or lost."

Slocum looked at him sharply. That sounded true. He too felt Jess was hitting on Dustin. Kept trying to make him draw. Hated for him to leave. Like he wanted hell-fire for the young cowboy to pull his gun.

"Why does he want your hide?" Slocum asked.

Dustin pulled a tobacco chew and bit off a piece. "Damned if I know. And he ain't the only one. Everyone wants my hide, I think. Ever since I left Red River." His brown eyes stared at Slocum. "Maybe I'm dreamin' it, but since Red River, I been shot at from ambush. Figured it was Apaches or drifters. They were slick. Shoot and run. Never got to see who in hell was shootin'." Dustin's face was grim. "I just wonder if somebody's got me on target."

Slocum shook his head. When someone shot at you on the trail, first you figured it was Apaches, then a drifter, then you felt yourself a target. That's how it went. Yet someone could be after him.

Dustin shook his head. "And here I am in a game in Lawson and someone's needling me to draw. Why?"

"Gamblers don't like losin' money, Dustin."

Dustin shrugged. "Maybe that's all it is."

Slocum stroked his chin and stared at the big sky. "You headed somewhere particular?"

"A ranch ten miles north of Tucson."

"What's there?"

Dustin's face was solemn, his voice husky. "My mother died a week ago. While she was dyin' she tole me I oughta go up to the Larrimore Ranch. It's my uncle, Steve Larrimore, who owns it."

"I heard of the Larrimore, it's big."

"I asked her, 'Why go now?' She says, 'Your dad died at Larrimore. It was a mystery what happened.'"

Dustin's face twisted with his memory of his mother on her deathbed. Then he went on. "She's breathin' hard, then says, 'I had to grab you, years ago, and run when your daddy got shot. Killin' by Apaches that night. Thought they were goin' to get you, too. I just knew if I didn't run with you, you'd be dead.'"

Dustin paused, looked away for a moment. "She's fightin' for breath. 'Didn't dare tell you 'bout this till now,' she says. 'I didn't want you leavin' me. But I'm finished. And it's time you dug up the truth. Go back to Larrimore.'"

"I said, 'For God's sake, to find out what, Mama? And why didn't you tell me long ago?'"

"She looked at me, a lot of love in her face, seemed about to talk, then she died."

Dustin's eyes glinted. "So that's where I'm goin', Slocum. I don't know why. But years ago, in Larrimore, when I was a kid, I remember a blond little girl, Millie. Bet she's grown into a beauty."

Slocum smiled, and curiously, he thought of the girl in the gorge he had saved two days ago. She too was a golden-haired beauty. He wondered if he'd ever see her again.

Dustin stared off at the riders, still small in the distance. "What are we gonna do, Slocum? Stand or run?"

Slocum looked at them riding hard. "They're not comin' to congratulate you for winning. They plan to string us up and take the money."

"Lot of bother for just a lousy pot."

That's what Slocum thought too. Nobody had gotten gunned down, yet they were coming with blood in their eyes. They wanted Dustin real bad. And Jim Hardy might be after Slocum's scalp for knocking off Red Hardy in Dodge. Slocum felt that Jim Hardy had recognized his name.

"Reckon we ought to try and discourage them," Slocum said.

"That'd be nice. How?"

Slocum sauntered to his roan and pulled out his Sharps. "This might do it," he said cheerfully.

Dustin laughed. "From here? You might hit the side of a mountain."

"Why don't we try."

They moved to a nearby crest of rocks. Dustin watched him, slightly amused. "Are you serious? Gonna fire from this distance? It's almost a mile."

"Mebbe I'll let them get a mite closer."

Dustin grinned. "Slocum, I respect you. You're a man who talks straight. But I can't believe you expect to hit anything from here." He cleared his throat. "If you do, I'll give you half of the pot I just won."

Slocum glanced at him. "Mighty generous. I might just take it."

He watched the five riders moving in a bunch, then got down on his stomach, leaned his rifle on a jutting rock, and stared through the sight.

Dustin watched, amused.

When Slocum fired, the rifle kicked, and he waited. The sound echoed off the cliffs. Nothing happened. Dustin studied the riders, who were still moving as a bunch. They kept moving. Dustin turned to Slocum, grinning. "Guess my money is safe."

"I didn't intend to hit anyone, just discourage them," Slocum said. Dustin turned to look at the riders again, to his eyes, mostly a blur in the shimmering heat. They had stopped. Dustin watched and thought. They had probably heard the bullet but couldn't figure where it came from and were studying the surroundings. Talking about it. Then, convinced that nobody was near, they started riding, following the trail left by Slocum and Dustin.

Dustin bit off a chew of tobacco and watched them. "They're comin' hard. To give us a stiff neck. I figger we oughta ride again."

Slocum glanced at him, then again leaned his rifle on the rock, aimed carefully, and squeezed the trigger. Dustin shook his head. The rifle crack echoed against the cliff. Again nothing happened. Dustin turned with a small smile. "That bullet ended up nowhere, Slocum. Impossible to hit a target from here. It's almost a mile. Hadn't we oughta start riding again?"

Slocum just kept looking at the bunch, and the glint in his green eyes made Dustin turn. There had been five riders, now there were four. They had stopped and were milling around.

Dustin was amazed. "Damn, you hit one. From here! Damn! If I hadn't seen it, I'd never have believed it."

Slocum stood up. "Reckon we can ride." He moved toward the horses. "They won't be in a hurry now."

Dustin kept staring into the distance. Then he turned and followed Slocum. They swung into their saddles and started to ride. "I heard of shootin' like that, but I never saw it."

Slocum said nothing, just looked ahead.

"Figure they'll stick with us, Slocum?"

"Depends on how much they want us."

The sun was starting to streak red in the sky when Slocum said, "If you're heading for Larrimore, you're going through Tucson."

"Right. The ranch is just north of Tucson."

"I'm going to Tucson too. Best if we rode together. These polecats aren't gonna let up so easy. 'Specially Jim Hardy. I think he knows I knocked his kin off."

"Why do you think that?"

"The look in his eye when he heard my name."

Dustin was solemn. "A mean dog, Jim Hardy. He's after my hide too."

Slocum nodded. "Hardy's the gun. But that guy Jess is the brain. Be interesting to know what's got *him* so fired up."

Dustin was thoughtful. "That's what I want to know. Jess Brady runs a scurvy bunch. A sore loser, you reckon?"

"Mebbe. I've seen plenty of drunk cowboys go hog-wild after they lose a big pot."

The sky reddened as the sun inched lower. They rode through high land, grassy land, long stretches of brush, rocks, and dry sand. They had no way of telling if they were still being trailed. They camped, made a fire, ate beef jerky and beans.

Afterward, Dustin pulled out a thin cigar. Slocum watched him light it. The slanting sunbeams hit Dustin's rugged face; he had a straight fine nose and a strong jaw. His brown eyes gazed at Slocum with friendliness. "Where you from, Slocum?"

"Georgia."

Dustin grinned. "You've come a long way from the old plantation."

Slocum nodded grimly, thinking of his beloved land, lost after the war, when a carpetbagger judge, brash and greedy, had dared to claim it.

No wonder he had exploded in violence: that carpetbagger's bones were now moldering under the earth. But it had made Slocum a wanderer in the territories of the West.

Dustin, aware that he had touched a sore point, became silent, and after they ate they rode southwest again under a flame-streaked sky. It was uneventful riding on a climbing trail that twisted through dense brush and trees, and after a time they came to a sudden clearing. That's when they saw two standing, saddled horses. Nearby a redheaded cowboy was bending over a man lying on the ground. The side of the man's face was bloody.

"Looks like the rider got thrown," Dustin said.

The redheaded cowboy saw them and raised a hand in friendly greeting. "Howdy. Hoss got spooked by a rattler and threw Sweeney. He's out. Got any whiskey?"

While Slocum watched, Dustin pulled the bottle from his saddlebag and brought it to the fallen man, who was wearing a short black hat over his eyes. He lay inert, the scrawl of blood on his cheek.

Dustin leaned down to bring the bottle to Sweeney's lips. As he did, the man's eyes suddenly opened, black, mischievous, and a gun came from the hand under his body. It pointed at Dustin.

"Howdy. Don't move, you or your friend, or I'll blast you to hell and back."

The redheaded cowboy turned to Slocum. "Drop your gun or the kid gets a bullet."

Slocum scowled. They were in a bad spot. It was a matter of split seconds—if he pulled his gun, he'd get Sweeney, but Dustin might be dead. He studied them. Who were they? Drifters out to scavenge, preying on lone riders or wagons from the East?

"What's all this?"

"Drop your gun, mister." There was hard threat in his voice.

"Fire your gun, you're dead," Slocum said.

"So's the kid."

He had the drop on Dustin, and it meant the kid's life. Maybe all they wanted was money. He'd take the chance.

He started for his holster.

"Easy now, no tricks."

Slocum dropped his gun.

Red rushed over to scoop it up. He had a fleshy face with a thick nose and a small mouth that twisted as he grinned. "Reckon we oughta tie 'em?"

"What for?" Sweeney said. He came forward, a narrow-faced, dark man with hooked nose and a sinewy body. "They make a move, we blast 'em."

"What do you want?" Slocum demanded. "Money?"

"Why not?" Sweeney grinned.

Slocum stared at him. "We give you the money, you let us ride?"

Red scowled. "Hey, mister, we're calling the shots."

"So let's see the money," Sweeney said, casually sticking the gun in his holster, confident he could pot them if they made a wrong move.

Slocum reached into his jeans and held out his buckskin wallet.

Sweeney scowled. "Just throw it here. You look tricky."

Actually, Slocum did have a trick in mind—grabbing the man's wrist when he reached for the money and going for his gun. But this dog was canny. Slocum tossed his wallet.

Sweeney turned to Dustin. "How 'bout you, kid? Turn it loose."

Dustin grimaced then sighed. "You hit it lucky, pardner. Just cleaned out a poker game." He too tossed his stuffed wallet.

Sweeney motioned to Red, who picked up the money. Gleefully he showed it to Sweeney. "Hey pal, didn't I tell you? Good things happen to bad guys."

Slocum looked grim, wondering if he'd made a mistake, and that he should have shot the balls off this joker when he could have. But Dustin would have gone down. "Hey, Sweeney. You got enough to keep you in whiskey and women for months. Can we ride? You got the guns, you can't get hurt."

Sweeney stared at him, and his lip curled. "I know you can't hurt us, mister. We pulled your teeth."

He turned to stare at Dustin. "What's your moniker?"

"Dustin."

"Dustin what?"

"What the hell's the difference?"

Sweeney moved close to Dustin and swung his fist. It knocked him down and bloodied his lip. "When I ask a question, answer it."

From the ground, Dustin's brown eyes glittered. "Dustin Larrimore."

There was silence. Sweeney didn't seem surprised, it

seemed to Slocum. There was grim satisfaction in his saturnine features.

"Kin to Steve Larrimore?"

Dustin scowled.

Red, standing alongside, kicked him with his boot. "Boy, you better learn to talk."

"Yeah, I'm kin."

Sweeney thoughtfully pulled a cigarillo and lit it.

Then Red swaggered in front of Slocum. "And who the hell are you?"

Slocum looked at Red's thick-featured face and felt like slamming it. But instead he said gently, "Slocum's the name, John Slocum."

Red's eyes narrowed, and he turned and walked to Sweeney and spoke in a low voice. "This Slocum's poison, Sweeney."

"What about him?"

"Heard about him in Hidalgo. Fancy gunwork during a saloon fight."

"So what? He's got no gun now."

"I don't like it."

"What the hell do you want to do?"

"Shoot the dog or turn him loose. He smells like trouble."

Sweeney turned to stare at the lean, powerful cowboy with the hard, green eyes. He did look dangerous. But nobody was dangerous without a gun. He could be dead meat in a minute.

"If we turn him loose, he might come back for the kid."

"Then shoot him."

Sweeney scowled. "When the time is right, I'll do what I have to. You worry too much."

Red's pale eyes blinked. "Hope you're doing this right, Sweeney."

Slocum watched them and wondered who they were. Though their duds were hard worn, they didn't look like drifters down to their last dime. Why were they playing a robber's game on the trail? And now that they had the money and guns, why didn't they just ride off?

Red picked up the whiskey bottle and took a long pull at it. "Might as well have a couple while we wait for Jess," he said.

Jess!

Dustin glanced secretly at Slocum, whose face had hardened. What the hell was happening? If these polecats had been with the Jess bunch, how in hell did they get here, out in front? Didn't seem possible. And he hadn't seen these men in the saloon at Lawson. They weren't in the saloon. If they had been, they would have known Dustin.

Slocum watched them drink and figured it might be smart to wait, that liquor loosened a man's tongue. And he had an ace to play, a throwing knife in the concealed pocket of his boot. Time was running out. Jim Hardy and his boys had to be riding hard. He'd have to do something fast.

Sweeney had got up and was going through Dustin's saddlebag. Red was watching Slocum, holding the bottle.

"Were you boys just out to scrounge what came along the trail? Or were you laying for us, Sweeney?"

A vague smile floated over his features. "You'd like to know that, Slocum?"

"Yeah. Want to know if it was fool's luck or if you're a couple of smart bozos."

Sweeney pulled a pair of field glasses from inside his

buckskin coat and stared down the valley to see four riders. A vague smile came to his face. "Just believe this, mister. We ain't dumb."

Slocum's mind raced. He looked at the trail from where these two polecats had come, a steep trail that from its top gave a hell of a view. Slocum's rifle shots had echoed off the cliffs. Alerted them. From the top they could have seen the whole valley, two horses pursued by a bunch. But how'd they know it was Jess Grady? Only if they had field glasses. It all fitted. Sweeney and Red were coming to join Jess in Lawson. And if Jess wanted these two hombres, they'd grab them.

Slocum lit a cigarillo. "You boys in Jess Grady's bunch?"

Red stared. "Why'd you ask that?"

"I know Jess. Knew him back in the ole days."

Sweeney glanced over, then went on digging in Dustin's saddlebag.

Red grinned suspiciously. "Yeah, what ole days? Where was that?"

"Knew him in Dodge City. Played poker with him."

Red's eyes flickered. "You knew him in Dodge, did yuh? Man, you talk with a forked tongue. Jess never was in Dodge."

He grinned viciously, and, thinking he had aced Slocum, turned to tell Sweeney they had a weasel liar in Slocum, when he heard a thin, strange whistle, then felt sharp agonizing pain. Suddenly his throat was blocked, he couldn't talk, and, in panic, his hands went up to his throat where he felt the cold steel of the throwing knife. He stumbled, trying to dig out the killing knife, not feeling the gun lifted from his holster. His strangled cry made Sweeney turn. In shock he saw the knife in Red's throat and behind him, Slocum with Red's gun in his hand. Sweeney grabbed at his holster, saw the spurt of fire from Slocum's gun, then everything went black in his brain.

Sweeney rocketed back with a hole in his forehead and fell, his dead eyes staring at the blood-red sky.

Slocum came forward quickly and pulled Dustin's gun from Sweeney's gunbelt and the wallets from his pockets. He tossed the gun to Dustin and started for the roan, which was picketed at a nearby grass patch.

Without a glance at the two fallen men, he said, "Let's make tracks. Grady's bunch must be coming on us fast."

Though their lead on the Jess Grady bunch was still good, they pushed the horses hard until sundown, when they found a good camping spot.

They made a fire in a deep pit, ate, and when they were drinking coffee, Dustin said, "Slocum, you're a rough hombre. Glad you're on my side."

Slocum said gently, "I'm just trying to survive in a tough territory." He sipped coffee. "I been thinking. You may be a target after all. These bozos seemed to want to trap us for Jess. And they had you in mind, Dustin."

Dustin's face was grim. "That's what I've felt all along." He cleared his throat. "Don't know who wants me. Jess? I ain't done anything to him."

"Might be someone else."

Dustin looked a bit pale.

Slocum thought about this fine rugged cowboy, a gutsy kid, alone against a vicious bunch of men. "Got a bit of fear, Dustin?"

Dustin laughed. "I don't like the odds. But you die only once."

Slocum grinned. "The smart thing is not to die in a hurry." He stroked his chin. "Would you like me to ride the trail with you to Larrimore?"

Dustin took a deep breath. "That would suit me a lot."

Slocum grinned. "Let's find out who's trying to make you mincemeat."

Dustin chewed on his lip. "Tell you the truth. If someone asked what in the whole world I want, I'd say, I'd want Slocum as a sidekick, while I went to find out what happened at Larrimore. How my dad got killed. Why my mother had to run. What she was feared to tell me. Solve the mystery of Larrimore."

Slocum emptied his cup on the fire. "We'll start at sunup."

3

Jess Grady stared into the distance and on a high slope could see the dim outlines of two riders. Headed for Tucson, just as he expected. He scowled, thinking about Dustin Larrimore.

Jess Grady felt he had been dumb about Dustin; he had played with him, like a spider with a fly, because he was so sure he had the kid in his web. He hadn't allowed that fate might step in by way of Slocum. That meddlesome cowboy had come out of the woodwork to spoil everything.

Jess had first noticed Slocum when he made Luke look like a fool, slamming him on his ass. Slocum looked tough, but Jess didn't want any bloody incidents. He had other things in mind. So when Jim Hardy had

gone over to settle it with Slocum, Jess told Jim to keep
the peace. That, Jess realized, had been a mistake. Jim
would have put a bullet in Slocum, and by now all
would be easy.

No, Jess didn't intend for Dustin to walk out of the
saloon breathing, not only because of his money. He
had a special reason. But Dustin got out because Slocum, cagy joker, had pulled his gun, positioned himself
behind Jim Hardy, and took control.

He grimaced, pulled a cigarillo, and thought about
Sweeney and Red, part of his bunch. They had been
studying the Tucson bank setup and were supposed to
join him in Lawson. Where the hell were they now?

He pulled his reins, and the bunch came around.
Frank Baker, Tim Brogan, Willie Stone, and Jim Hardy,
all tough guns, seasoned fighters who had been through
plenty with him.

"We'll give the horses a breather," Jess said.

Jim Hardy didn't look happy; he didn't care about
horses. He wanted Slocum in the worst way. They
swung off their saddles, took out their canteens, and sat
around.

"Listen," Jess said. "One of those jokers, I think it's
Slocum, has a Sharps, and he can use it. We won't be
able to get in close. But they're headed for Tucson, so
we'll get them. But the main thing is the bank."

"Where the hell are Sweeney and Red?" asked Tim
Brogan, a black-haired, sinewy man with a knife scar
on his cheek. "They were s'posed to catch up with us in
Lawson."

"Red's got a taste for booze. It probably slowed them
down," said Willie Stone, a wiry gunman with a broken
nose. He grinned.

"Probably on the trail now," said Jess. "We'll run into them."

"It's Slocum I want," said Jim Hardy.

"Who the hell *is* this Slocum?" asked Jess.

"I saw him once in Tombstone 'bout a month ago," said Willie.

They all turned to look at him.

"What do you know about him?" asked Jess.

Willie pulled out a plug of tobacco and bit off a chew. "I don't know who he is, but I seen him in action. I was drinking at the bar, and there was a cardsharp called Fast Eddie, ripping off the players. He was a quick gun, and nobody dared call him. Then Slocum sits down, and after a couple of pots, Slocum calls him crooked. Fast Eddie curses and tries to come up with a derringer. Slocum grabs his arm and flattens him with a punch. Fast Eddie gets up, foaming. He calls for a shoot-out.

"They go out in the street, everyone watching. Fast Eddie says he's willin' to forget it if Slocum apologizes. Slocum says Fast Eddie is still crooked, and while he's talkin', slippery Eddie jerks his gun, but Slocum put a bull's-eye in Fast Eddie's head." Willie squirted tobacco juice. "Quite a show."

There was silence.

Jim Hardy had listened with a stony face. "So what? I've seen Eddie. They called him 'Fast,' but there was molasses in his draw. I'm looking for a shot at Slocum."

"You'll get it," said Jess. "But we don't take dumb risks. We keep this bunch together by being smart. We'll pick up these boys in Tucson. The bank is the main thing."

They mounted up and started riding again.

• • •

They rode for a while, following Dustin and Slocum's trail, until they reached the slope, which they climbed cautiously. Then they saw the buzzards circling overhead, and Jess Grady's mouth tightened. What was the carcass—human or animal?

They rode fast until they came to the clearing and saw the two sprawled bodies.

The men pulled up their horses and stared.

Red with a knife wound in his throat, his shirt soaked in blood. And Sweeney with a bullet hole in the middle of his forehead.

The men stared silently, then Willie Stone said. "Bull's-eye. That's Slocum's kind of shootin'."

Jess turned to Frank Baker, who had been an Army scout, trained by a Cherokee. "What d'ya make of this, Frank?"

Frank swung off his saddle and examined the ground carefully. After a while, he said, "Looks like Sweeney had these two mutts pinned down. May have got their guns. But he didn't get someone's throwing knife. That did it."

Jess Grady's voice was hard. "Had to be Slocum. Not the sort of thing Dustin could do." He stared at the two dead men. "So now we've lost Sweeney and Red."

He turned, grim-faced. "We're goin' to take good care of this Slocum. But keep this in mind, we treat him like dynamite. You hear me? Now pull your shovels and bury 'em."

4

Tucson was baking in the sun when Slocum and Dustin rode down Main Street. They stopped at the hitch rail in front of the Parson's General Store and walked into the cool interior.

Slocum ordered beef jerky, coffee, and canned beans. "How much?"

"Two dollars." Parson, the proprietor, was a dark-haired man with a pink, fleshy face. He kept staring at Dustin until Slocum, who noticed, said, "What's biting you, mister?"

Parson looked confused. "Sorry, didn't realize I was starin'. But this young man looks just like a customer who used to ride round here years ago."

"Who would that be?" Dustin asked.

"Man called Amos Larrimore."

Slocum looked sharply at Dustin.

Just then the door opened and a girl stood at the threshold, the sun, from the back, illuminating her golden hair. Something about her hit Slocum, and when she stepped inside, he realized why. It was the blond girl in the canyon who had been attacked by two gunmen.

She glanced at him, but no recognition showed in her blue eyes. "Hello, Mr. Parson. Perhaps you have our groceries ready."

"Been waitin' for you, Miss Millie." He pulled out two paper bags filled with canned goods. She glanced at a pert little pink bonnet hanging on a peg and, on impulse, put it on her head.

"That's right purty, Miss Millie," said Mr. Parson.

She smiled brightly as she stood in front of the small round mirror to set it properly.

Slocum and Dustin looked at the girl as she fixed it.

"Ever seen anything as nice, Dustin?" Slocum asked.

At the name, the girl turned sharply and stared at Dustin. "Dustin?" she said and moved close to look at him. "I do declare, you must be Dustin Larrimore. That brat of a boy. All growed up."

Dustin's eyes gleamed, then his face cracked in a broad grin. "And you must be Millie Walker, that brat of a tomboy, all growed up."

They stared at each other and laughed.

"Hard to believe what time has done to you, Millie. You used to be a freckled, scrawny little thing," Dustin said, admiring her full figure.

She smiled. "That's what time does. You're far from that nasty noisy, pesky brat."

Slocum couldn't help smiling, looking at them. Fine strong specimens of the West.

Then the girl, curious about Dustin's companion, looked keenly at Slocum. "And I must say, mister, you look familiar, though I'm not sure I know you."

Slocum smiled. "The misfortune is mine, Miss Millie. Slocum is the name."

She looked charmed by his Southern gallantry. Her eyes stayed on him, jogged by a memory she couldn't fix. But her mind went back to Dustin. "You and your mother went off awful sudden," she said, looking puzzled. She turned to Slocum. "My dad, Dave Walker, is foreman of the Larrimore Ranch. And I saw a lot of Dustin when we were kids, Mr. Slocum. Fought like wildcats. Then one day, he and his ma disappeared. Never knew what happened to them. Dad wouldn't talk about it. And Steve Larrimore never mentioned them. Mighty strange."

Her lovely eyes gazed at Dustin steadily. "And here you are. Whatever happened to you? And your mother, where's she?"

Dustin's face became somber. "Ma's dead. Died last week. Told me to go to the Larrimore Ranch." His eyes grew steely. "To see my uncle," he added.

Millie stared at him, her eyes troubled. But whatever it was, she didn't speak of it.

"Something's happening round here lately. Mean hombres making trouble. A couple of days ago, Bart, one of our hands, was riding with me in Duras Canyon and two gunmen came down on us. Shot Bart dead. They'd of had me, too, but..." She stopped, and suddenly turned to Slocum. "It was you, wasn't it? I was looking up at the sun. Couldn't get too clear a view. But there was something about you. It was you who did the shooting!"

Slocum smiled. "I was there."

"Well, Mr. Slocum, you saved my life. God knows what would have happened." She turned to Dustin. "Two quick shots, that did it."

"Who were they? What'd they want?" Slocum asked.

"They wanted me to come along with them. They had been waiting for me, I'm sure. Bart told them over his dead body. They argued, then one of them shot him. I think they were going to kidnap me. For money? I don't know."

Slocum looked at Dustin and shook his head. Odd things were happening. He wondered if they fitted together or were just strange and unconnected.

He had the feeling they were moving deeper into the mystery the closer they got to the Larrimore Ranch.

Just then a husky, apple-cheeked boy pushed open the door screen, came in and gazed at Millie in the pink bonnet. "You sure look nice, Miss Millie." He went toward the bags of groceries and lifted them. "I'll put these in the wagon."

"My cousin Seth." She smiled. "This is Dustin Larrimore. You heard me talk of him. And his friend, Mr. Slocum."

Seth nodded, his blue eyes saucer-wide as he stared at Dustin.

Millie went on, "Dustin, I'm sorry to hear about your ma. I'm sure my dad and your uncle will be glad to see you."

She turned to the proprietor, who had been busy putting sundries in their cubbyholes. "As for this bonnet, Mr. Parson, let me think about it. Might get it for the dance." She put the bonnet back on the peg, and turned, looking coquettishly at Dustin and Slocum. "Hope you gentlemen will find time to come to our Midsummer Dance. It brings the pretty girls in from miles around."

And with a flirtatious toss of her blond curly hair, she followed Seth out the door.

After Slocum and Dustin had put their supplies in their saddlebags, they went into Lucy's Cafe, where they had coffee and biscuits.

"Very pretty girl," said Slocum.

"As a kid, she was a roughneck, always trying to get one up on me." Dustin grinned. "So you saved her skin, too. Mighty lucky to have you nearby, Slocum."

Slocum remembered the two ruffians as they shot her friend Bart down in cold blood. They shot Millie's horse, then they knocked her around. He looked grim. "Some men are better off dead."

He looked out the window at Main Street, where cattlemen and a few hard-looking, sleazy cowboys were loafing. The sound of hooves hitting the ground hard made them turn to look down the street.

A sturdy wagon pulled by four horses came thundering up, escorted by five horsemen in dusty uniforms. As the driver brought the Wells Fargo wagon to a stop in front of the Tucson Bank, the cloud of dust that had been following the wagon and riders roiled around and then began to disperse.

The dusty riders were big, brawny, and packed big hardware. They leaped from their saddles, eyed everyone suspiciously, and stood guard with shotguns in front of the bank. Three men in shirtsleeves came out of the bank, pulled a heavy strongbox out of the wagon, and, escorted by one broad-shouldered man, lugged it into the bank.

The men nearby looked on with intense interest.

Finally, the rider stalked out of the bank, looked keen-eyed at the nearby spectators, then snapped an order. The guards jumped on their horses, the driver cracked his whip, and the wagon, springs creaking loudly, plunged ahead, escorted by three riders in front and two behind, an impregnable force.

Slocum had watched it all, amused; money made a town nervous. The sleazy men started to chatter. Clearly, money in the bank dazzled their minds.

Slocum sipped his coffee and was glancing idly through the window, when his eye picked up the brown-haired young woman sauntering down the street. She wore a sleek yellow dress that clung tightly to her full figure. She had a well-packed bosom that jounced with the movement of her curly hair. Slocum was enjoying the sight of her when he suddenly recognized her. Her name was Marylou, and he'd known her in Forked River. She was a sizzler on the mattress.

Slocum glanced at Dustin and did some quick thinking. "Listen, Dusty, take the horses to the livery and get them grained. Let the smithy look at their shoes."

Something in Slocum's tone astonished Dustin. "And what are you goin' to do?"

"I've got some business to attend to, and I'll get rooms at the hotel."

"What business?"

"I just told you." He kept staring through the window. "Think I see an old friend."

"Who the hell would that be?"

Slocum threw him a hard look. "You're a nosy kid. That girl out there. I expect to renew old acquaintance."

Dustin stared out and looked impressed by Marylou's lush figure. "Wouldn't mind makin' her acquaintance."

"Run along, Dustin. The livery."

Dustin groused and went out the cafe toward the horses.

Slocum watched Marylou walk from the boardwalk across the street and come toward Lucy's Cafe.

His eyes raked her figure as she came closer, her lush breasts, the print of her nipples on her yellow dress, the long slender waist and full hips. It put him in mind of how she looked under the dress, back in Forked River, and he felt a jump in his britches.

He expected her to come into the cafe, but it looked like she was going past it. Her dark brown eyes glanced in the window and she saw him. She frowned, then her face smiled radiantly. She watched him get up, drop money on the table, and come out the door.

"My God, John Slocum. What are you doin' in Tucson? D'ya mind if I kiss you right here."

He glanced at some cowboys loafing nearby. "Maybe you could hold off a few minutes."

"Hold off?" Her pretty face looked puzzled.

"That's all it takes to get to the hotel room."

The dark eyes in her nicely modeled face brightened. "I see. That's the nicest thing that's happened today."

The room in the hotel had a big bed, an oak chair, a table, and a bureau with a washbasin. From the desk clerk downstairs, he had bought a bottle, and now he poured two glasses of whiskey.

She quaffed half of her drink.

"I see you still have a strong thirst," he said.

"I like hard liquor and a hard man," she drawled.

He smiled. "Well, here's the liquor and here's the man."

She laughed, raising her drink. "It's nice to know. So Slocum, what are you doin' in Tucson?"

"Rode in with a pardner named Dustin. Going to his uncle's ranch. The Larrimore."

"Steve Larrimore? One of the big ranchers. Big herds of cattle. He ships to Kansas." Something about her tone got him.

"You know the man?"

She chose her words carefully. "Know him, yes. He's rich, he's powerful. You know how they are. But he seems like a courtly man."

"Well, he's just about to renew an acquaintance with his kin, Dustin."

She looked thoughtful. "Larrimore has no wife and no kids. He's gonna need someone to take over someday."

"It may be a good thing for Dustin," Slocum said.

They drank in silence.

Then she said, "Are we goin' to sit here and talk, or do you have something else in mind?"

He laughed, went to her, and held her lush body tight. He stroked her full buttocks, pleasuring in their round firmness. He slipped his hand into the cut of her dress and held one of her plump silky breasts, feeling the erect nipple. Her kissed her. Then he peeled his clothes off.

She gazed at his proud flesh. "So you did have something else in mind."

Her body was better than he remembered. Slender, long-waisted, with full, voluptuous hips and finely shaped legs and thighs. His hands roamed over her body, over the shapely breasts. She reached for his arousal.

They did nice things to each other, and he carried her

to the bed. She pulled at his body, his hands stroked the smooth flesh. Her thighs came apart, and he moved into the velvet of her and felt the pleasure. She caught his rhythm and clasped his waist. He drove strong and vigorously until he felt the jolt of her body. He paused to let her enjoy it, then continued to drive until he reached his peak, a surge of pleasure. After a brief respite, they did it again.

When Dustin came to the hotel later he found Slocum in the bed, hands behind his head, gazing reflectively out the window at a star-studded Arizona sky. Dustin saw the bottle and poured a drink. "I took care of the horses," he said.

Slocum nodded.

Dustin looked at the wrecked bed. "And you took care of your business."

Slocum turned to the sinewy young cowboy. The kid had a bite to his humor. "Yes, I took care of it."

Dustin sipped his drink. "Wish I had business like that to take care of."

Slocum grinned. "You're a horny brat. Didn't think you were so ready to run away from Millie, your childhood sweetie."

Dustin's eyes widened. "Sweetie? She'd sooner kick me than kiss me."

Slocum smiled. "That's how the ladies handle men— kissing and kicking."

Dustin laughed. "A man of your experience would know." He looked solemn. "They tell me my uncle comes into town."

"Larrimore was your father's brother?"

"Younger brother." Dustin bit his lip. "Mama told me

he was the tough one. Hard to control. But later he turned around, steadied."

"Well," Slocum said, "I've heard that he's got no kids, no wife. All he's got is a big ranch and a big herd of cattle. I reckon he should be happy to find himself some kin."

Dustin's eyes closed. "Never know. Best not to have expectations. I've learned that in my short life."

"You've learned fast."

Dustin sipped his drink. "Main thing is to get answers. Like how Dad died that night. Never got the whole story. Uncle Steve oughta know."

"Apache attack, you said."

"That was it. I want to hear about it."

Slocum looked into the smoldering eyes of Dustin Larrimore, and he could read the seething feelings. Dustin was unsatisfied with the story of his father's death. But his mother had never talked about it until she was on her deathbed. It was strange. Well, they were on their way to the Larrimore Ranch.

Maybe he'd find answers. And again, maybe he'd find trouble.

5

The sun blazed in the hot blue sky, and the dust stirred behind Slocum as his boots hit the street. He walked past the general store, where shoppers were laying supplies on their wagons, past the bank, where two uniformed guards at the door eyed him curiously, past the livery, where the smith clanked on his anvil. Finally he came to Sam's Barber Shop. His hair had grown long and needed cutting. He opened the screen door, and the barber, Sam, gazed at him. He was a smiling, amiable man with a black crop of hair, and he was working on a brawny customer in the chair whose face was lathered up. Sam paused, holding his razor, and stared at Slocum, his eyes flashing with recognition.

Slocum picked up on something and alerted. It would

45

be wise, he thought, not to expose himself to Sam's razor until he found out what had ticked him off. He had no recognition of the man, but Slocum's instinct did not suggest danger needlessly.

"You look long overdue at a barber," Sam said.

Slocum smiled. "Well, Mr. Sam, a good barber is hard to find."

"You come to the right place," Sam said, grinning. "Where you riding in from?"

"From Lawson."

"Lots of strangers drifting into town lately," Sam said.

The man in the chair spoke up. "Wouldn't surprise me, Sam, if the bank delivery hasn't brought out a lot of hopefuls."

Sam shook his head. "Don't know about that. This town's not a good place for robbers. A batch of 'em pushing daisies in Boot Hill. Our bank man, Mr. Barnes, has smart guns protecting his bank money."

The man in the chair chuckled. "There's always a gunman who thinks he's smart enough to crash the bank."

"Won't happen here," said Sam as he stroked the lather on the man's face.

Slocum was curious about the customer but couldn't tell much, except he was brawny and that Sam treated him with respect.

Sam turned to Slocum. "Believe I've seen you before, mister."

Slocum smiled genially. "Where would that be, Sam?"

"Missouri. Been to Missouri?"

Slocum looked solemn as he thought of his guerrilla days of riding with Bill Quantrill. "Yes, I been there."

Sam stared at him. "Rode with Quantrill. Right?"

Slocum looked carefully at the man. No hostility in his face. There were men who'd pull their gun if they knew you rode with the Quantrill Raiders.

"Yes, I rode with him."

"Saw you in the saloon that one night. You boys were celebrating. Knocked off a big bunch of bluecoats, guerrilla style of fightin'. Ambush, hit and run." Sam shook his head, and his voice was solemn as he spoke to his customer. "And I'll never forget that night. I saw them: Quantrill, Bloody Bill Anderson, Jesse James, Cole Younger. And you were there. It was a night of history."

Slocum thought of the time, and he remembered the riding, the hiding, the shooting, and the dying. He had been younger then, and fighting for the Cause.

"Some of the best guns came out of that bunch," said Sam.

"Some of the great outlaws, after the war, came out of that bunch," said the customer.

It was true, Slocum thought, and he wondered again about the man in the chair.

Sam grinned. "They sure got the best training on how to rob a bank. Hit and run."

There was silence while Sam toweled the lather off the man's face. He sat up, an older man, powerful presence, big shoulders, a strong nose in a rugged face, shrewd dark brown eyes.

He turned to Slocum. "I heard about Bloody Bill Quantrill," his voice was husky. "A man with a heart of stone. I don't know who you are, mister. But I'm sorry to hear you rode with that killer. Well, that was a time ago."

There was a pause. Then Slocum said, "I'll tell you

about Quantrill, mister. He was a man who didn't know the meaning of defeat. And defeat was all the South had in those days. That's what attracted the men who rode with him."

The man rubbed his smooth face, then got off the chair. He was bigger than Slocum. He reached for his Stetson and put it on his head. He wore a frock coat, a brown vest, and well-fitting striped trousers. He had an air of self-confidence. "So you're one of those who don't know the meaning of defeat? Must say I like that in a man. May I ask your name, sir?"

"Slocum, John Slocum."

"I'm Steve Larrimore. I've got a spread some miles north of here. You might be looking for work. If so, we'll find something for you."

"Didn't think you cared for the Quantrill riders," Slocum said.

"Let bygones be bygones," Larrimore said. Then a strange smile came to his lips. "Surprising what a man will do if he believes hard in something."

Slocum looked intently into Larrimore's brown eyes. There was no resemblance between this man and Dustin. Yet he had to be a brother to Dustin's father.

Larrimore looked in the mirror and turned to the barber. "Well, you've done your usual damage, Sam." He grinned and pulled out some money. He nodded to Slocum and strode out the door.

Slocum watched him, a strong, confident man, a wealthy man who knew what he wanted. He had carved out a great prize in the territory for himself.

Somehow Slocum had felt no inclination to tell Larrimore that his nephew had come out to see him.

He wondered why.

• • •

Slocum sat in the barber's chair and watched Sam cut his shaggy locks.

"This Larrimore talks like a big man," Slocum said.

"The biggest," said Sam. "It's a compliment if Larrimore offers you a job."

"Why so?"

"He picks the best. Pays top money." Sam grinned. "The work is risky."

"Risky?"

"He keeps a hard bunch for gun work. He's a rich man. And there are rustlers who want his cattle, outlaws who want his money." Sam sighed. "It's a known fact in this world, if you got chickens, the foxes will come to steal."

Slocum grinned. "So you give two bits of philosophy with your haircuts."

"No extra charge," chuckled Sam, snipping with his scissors.

Slocum smiled and looked in the mirror, which reflected the street. He could see a cowboy driving a wagon, a woman waiting near Lucy's Cafe, and two burly men going into the bank. They looked familiar.

Sam stood back to admire his work. "Look at that cut—a work of art."

Slocum examined his hair and grinned. "Well, I feel five pounds lighter. And you're not a butcher who's lost his way." He gave the barber a fine tip, walked out to the sunbaked street, and headed for the saloon, where he expected to meet Dustin.

It was payday, and cowpunchers, in from outlying ranches for drinking and fun, crowded the saloon. There was noise and smoke, drinkers at the bar, and hard-faced men gambling at the tables. The town pulled in cattlemen, drifters, outlaws, and gunmen. You didn't know who you were rubbing elbows with.

He saw Dustin playing poker with five men, and, in a mood to relax, Slocum worked his way to the crowded bar. As he waited for the busy barkeep he glanced around. It was a rough, smoky, playful atmosphere, with several women lolling about, talking to the men. The girls wore flouncy dresses that showed plenty of bosom and legs.

He glanced again at Dustin and was amused to see how carefully he held his cards and studied the other players. As a gambler Dustin had a natural shrewdness.

Slocum felt easy, though he had to keep in mind that Jess Grady and his bunch might come stomping into town. Of course, they might have a deal on elsewhere.

The barkeep, who the men called Smitty, came up. He was barrel-bellied, with a pink, parched face that showed he favored the product he served.

"What'll it be, mister?" His pale blue eyes glanced shrewdly at the lean, sinewy, dangerous-looking stranger in the brown vest and Stetson.

"Whiskey."

After he poured the glass, he lingered curiously for a moment. "Riding through?"

"You never know." Slocum smiled easily. He'd known a lot of men who thought they were riding through, but on the way got planted in the town cemetery.

"No, you never know." Smitty smiled grimly. He, too, had seen many calamities, many of them starting and ending in his saloon.

Slocum downed his drink and poured another as the barkeep went off to other customers.

The whiskey eased him, and he felt content. Looking around, he noticed a well-built woman with a pretty face smiling at him.

She came toward him. "Well, hi," she said, "I'm Margo."

"Slocum."

"You look like a man who'd be fun to know."

He thought of the hectic hours he'd just spent with Marylou and sighed. "To be honest, I fear I'm clean out of bullets. But I sure like the look of you, Margo."

She seemed disappointed. "Hate to find you like that."

He laughed. It was not a good time, anyway, to go sporting with a woman when the Grady bunch could well stomp in. He'd hate to be caught with his pants down.

"I always hate to put off for tomorrow what I can take today. It's a chancy life," Margo said.

Slocum scowled. It seemed true enough. You push away a lady of pleasure, and in the next hour, in your death throes, you might have time to regret it. He looked at her curves, and they were plenty, and he wondered if he should reconsider.

While he was thinking, some drunk nearby shot his gun at the ceiling.

Everyone turned to look. He was a cocky, bewhiskered cowboy in a blue shirt, whose face was red with drink. He looked happy but slightly nutty. He was nearby, and Slocum's eyes narrowed—drunks like that, with brains soaked in whiskey, could be dangerous.

"All right," the drunk yelled in his whiskey voice. "I want you polecats talkin' to the ladies to step back, so's I kin see 'em. I want to see the ladies. So step back, you

critters, you hear me." And he punctuated his command
with shots at the ceiling.

He sounded comic but crazy, and the men talking to
the women, aware that in his befuddled state he might
throw wild bullets, hastily stepped away. The women
looked startled and delighted at the fun of it, but nervous, too.

Slocum, who was close to the cowboy, held his
drink. It wasn't the first time he'd seen booze hit a
man's head like that. This one wanted all the women,
and he figured he had the weapon to get what he
wanted. A real nut.

The cowboy grinned as he saw his order obeyed, and
his eyes roved over the crowd until he saw Slocum, who
hadn't moved, and Margo, who was still standing next
to him. The cowboy's face hardened, and he swung his
gun around.

Smitty the barkeep spoke up. His eyes were worried,
but he kept his tone pleasant. "Now, Lem. Simmer
down. Put your gun up. There's plenty of girls here for
you."

Lem shot another bullet at the ceiling. "Shet yo'
face, Smitty." He swaggered over to Slocum, his gun
pointing, his face in a weird mix of comic threat. "Hey,
cowboy—are you deef? Didn't you hear me?"

Slocum was still holding his drink, and he smiled.
"Didn't hear a thing, mister. What was it you were saying?"

As the cowboy struggled to think about that, Slocum
tossed his drink into the man's eyes, blinding him for
the instant needed to grab the drunk's wrist and get the
gun from his hand.

It almost cracked the cowboy's wrist, and he whim-
pered with pain.

A big laugh went up, and a couple of barmen hustled Lem outside to the water trough to cool him down. The men around smiled at Slocum, and the bar went back to normal.

"You did that nicely, mister," said Margo, flashing her eyes. "When you're feeling romantic, come and see me. You won't be sorry."

"Reckon I won't," Slocum said.

He started toward Dustin's card table, where one player had stood up. "I'm through," he said disgustedly. "My luck is running bad."

It left an open seat, and Slocum, curious how Dustin handled his cards, spoke up. "Mind if I sit in?"

"I don't mind," said Dustin, glancing innocently at the other players. "Always room for another sucker."

The players were startled at such a remark, tossed casually at this lean, powerful, green-eyed stranger. Especially one with the cool nerve to handle drunken Lem at the bar. But surprisingly the stranger took no offense, smiling easily as he sat down. He said modestly, "It won't be the first time I've had my feathers plucked."

Slocum was amused to note that Dustin again looked a winner; most of the money was stacked in front of him. After a few pots, Slocum could understand why Dustin was a winner. He was a slow study and seemed able to figure the odds, when to stay in and when to bluff.

The door swung open and there was a rustle at the bar. Slocum glanced up and saw Jim Hardy and a high-cheeked, broken-nosed gunman swagger through the crowd to the bar. The men there gave Jim Hardy, a feared gunman, plenty of space. With a broad grin,

Smitty, the barkeep, poured two whiskies and slapped down the bottle. "Hi, Jim. How goes it?"

The gunman, in a sullen mood, just grunted, belted his booze, and poured himself another. Interested in drinking, he hadn't yet seen Slocum or Dustin. When he talked, he spoke to the gunman with him.

Slocum's chair faced the bar, and he played casually. Dustin was dealing, and to his pleasure Slocum picked up a pair of aces. Not wanting to scare off the other players, he bet modestly. But one of the others, Hogan, a red-faced, beefy man with narrow brown eyes, felt he had good cards and came on strong.

Then Hardy saw Slocum and his eyes widened. "Looks like we're in luck, Willie," said Hardy. "I tole you, if you wait long enough, you always catch up with a buzzard."

"What buzzard you got in mind this time, Jim?" asked Willie Stone, who had been facing the bar.

"The buzzard is playin' poker." He smiled grimly. "This time he won't be able to pull a gun in back of a man."

Then Willie saw Slocum and Dustin, and he grinned. In Willie's mind Slocum was already a candidate for Boot Hill. He and Hardy had been in the Grady bunch for almost a year, and he'd seen Hardy pull his gun, time after time. And Jim Hardy's gun always spit death. He wore his Colt low, to where his hand hung, not to lose an instant. The trigger had been honed to a hairsbreadth touch. And Jim Hardy was built sinewy, the ideal gunfighter body. To Willie he was the top gunfighter in this territory, though maybe he could be matched by Billy the Kid. It was true that Willie had seen Slocum draw in Tombstone, where he had hit Fast Eddie. And Slocum was no slouch. But Willie had seen

Hardy mow down too many men, all breeds, and it would be no different now. He could see Slocum already in a pine box. Slocum had shot Hardy's brother. And in Lawson, he caused Hardy a loss of dignity, something unforgivable.

He waited for Hardy to make his move.

In the meantime, Slocum had picked up two queens for a double pair. Dustin and the others dropped out, and the betting between Hogan and Slocum became serious. It caught the attention of the men in the saloon, and Slocum noticed Jim Hardy's eyes widen and a grim smile settle on his lips. Hardy then made his move, sauntering toward the card table, followed by Willie.

Figuring it might be smart to bring the betting to a halt, in case of sudden unpleasantness, Slocum met Hogan's last raise.

Men had gathered around the table to watch, but they parted to let Jim Hardy move in close. His eyes gleamed as he saw the winnings in front of Dustin. Then his gaze settled hawklike on Slocum.

Hogan showed kings and tens, and he grinned, anticipating a win. But Slocum laid down his aces and queens and raked in the pot. "It's called the luck of the draw," he said to Hogan pleasantly.

"Some call it luck, some call it cheatin'," said Jim Hardy in a harsh voice, standing still.

The men nearby stiffened and moved quickly toward the walls, aware that Jim Hardy, the fastest gun, was about to put on a show. Dustin kept his seat. Hogan, too, stayed put, puzzled. "Why say that, Hardy? I didn't see anything wrong here."

"I've seen this kid and this joker Slocum. I think you got fleeced, Hogan."

Hogan scowled. "I don't know about that, Hardy. I

can spot a sharper quick as anyone. And these cards were dealt fair."

Jim Hardy's tone was cold. "Don't cross me, Hogan."

Hogan paled, and his lips tightened.

Slocum stood up slowly. "Thank you, Hogan. I play honest poker. But Jim Hardy craves a showdown, though he has no cause that I can see."

Hardy's mouth was tight. "I got cause aplenty, Slocum. You shot my brother in Dodge. Probably shot him when he wasn't looking, the kinda man you are."

Slocum eyes were like green ice. "Your brother was a drunken slob who liked to push people around. I reckon it runs in the family."

There was a gasp from some spectators who knew Hardy's rep as an unbeatable gunslinger.

Jim Hardy himself could scarcely believe his ears. Nobody had ever dared talk like that to him. His face twisted with fury and his hand flashed to his gun, his famous lightning draw, and he fired, but he missed because he was already dead. Slocum's bullet had pierced his forehead and came out spattering brains.

Slocum studied the broken-nosed gunman who had come in with Hardy, never dreaming he'd need help. Now he was staring shocked at Jim Hardy, dead on the floor.

"Throw your gun," Slocum ordered.

Pale-faced, Willie threw it.

Slocum gazed at the crowd. They watched him, and seemed to be holding their breath. Nobody looked hostile.

He holstered his gun.

"I'll just pick up my winnings," he said.

6

Jess Grady looked at two buzzards winging across the light-streaked sky, and to him they appeared to be in a hurry. Somewhere death was waiting for them. There were times when Grady felt kinship with the buzzard, because he too found himself often in the presence of death. Men died around him. For a moment, he thought of Steve Larrimore and smiled.

He brought the whiskey bottle to his lips, took a long pull, then held it out to Frank Baker, who was sitting near him.

Jess Grady and Frank Baker had a camp fire going two miles south of Tucson, and they had just finished eating when Grady sighted Willie Stone on his sorrel riding hard over the crest. From the look of Willie's riding, Jess expected bad news; he had an instinct for such things.

Willie jumped from his horse, slapped the dust off his hat, and took the bottle from Frank Baker's hands and drank deeply. His dark eyes gleamed in his scarred face with its broken nose.

"You've got a strong thirst, Willie," said Frank softly.

Willie just wiped his mouth and took another pull.

"Did you case the bank?" asked Jess in a quiet voice.

Willie handed the bottle back to Baker. "I cased it. Two guards inside, two outside."

"That's okay. What we need is surprise," said Jess. "There's a cafe nearby. Jim Hardy will work from there on the mutts outside. After we go into the bank, he'll shoot their balls off."

Frank nodded. "Sounds good."

But Willie said nothing, just stared at the crackling fire and the tin cups and empty plates next to it. Jess stared at him. "Reckon Jim Hardy's in place. Waitin' for us."

Willie looked grim. "Oh, he's in place, all right. But he ain't waitin'."

Jess scowled. "What the hell's that mean?"

Willie Stone faced him. "Hate to tell you this, Jess. Jim Hardy, fastest gun in these parts, has just met a faster gun."

There was a heavy silence.

"Someone beat his draw?" Jess said, incredulous.

"Yeah," said Willie.

"Who the hell was it?"

"Slocum."

Frank Baker glowered. "You tellin' this straight, Willie?"

"I was there. And Slocum didn't want the draw. Hardy pushed for it."

The fire crackled in the silence.

"You saw him beat?" Jess glared. "And you didn't back him up?"

"Never dreamed it would happen. I was gapin' like a fish on a hook. Slocum turned on me. Made me drop my gun."

Jess cursed viciously. "There it is. I told him that Slocum was dynamite. But Hardy was always a hard head. Had to prove himself the best."

Frank spoke slowly. "Slocum shot Hardy's brother in Dodge, Jess. Reckon that was eating on Hardy's gut."

Jess took the whiskey bottle. "All right. He had a hate on Slocum. Wants him dead. A bullet in the back makes Slocum dead. Hardy didn't have to put his life on the line. You know all about that, Willie."

Willie Stone nodded. He was one of the best back-shooters in the business.

Jess Grady smiled maliciously as he looked at the two men. "It's the smart guy who stays alive, not the bravest." He pulled out a cigarillo and lit it while his men watched. "So there's Jim Hardy. He pulled his gun against Slocum after I warned him. Now he's goin' to be the bravest polecat in the cemetery."

He puffed his cigarillo thoughtfully. "We'll ride into town tomorrow. We've got three deals ahead. Dustin Larrimore and the bank—that's the money. Slocum's the gun. We'll figure out how to take care of that."

Jess and his men were riding a high crest in the hilly country when they heard a gunshot. They dismounted, crawled to the edge of the rocks, and, looking over, spotted the Tucson stagecoach, halted below on the trail between narrow cliffs. Two men in masks were collecting money from four male passengers and a woman. A third masked rider, holding his gun, watched them from a spirited black horse.

Jess studied the situation, then grinned. "That's Bullethead and his boys, Mike and Lorry."

"Robbing the stage, as usual," said Willie.

Jess shook his head. "Penny-ante robbers. Bullethead never had the imagination for hitting the big stuff."

In silence they watched one gunman go into the coach, looking for hidden valuables.

Jess looked thoughtful. "I figure that we're ridin' short. We lost a big gun in Hardy. We need new blood. We could bring these boys into our bunch. We need more guns to hit the Tucson bank. What d'ya think of it?"

"Not much, Jess," said Willie, scowling. "The more men, the smaller the split. We can handle this, we three. We've done it before."

Jess stroked his chin. "Well, Willie, there's four guards, and we don't know what stray gun we may run into. We need strong backup, just in case." He turned to Frank.

"Won't hurt to have them along," said Frank.

"I'm saying it might hurt afterward, when we come to divvy," said Willie, his mouth tight.

A secret smile twisted Jess Grady's mouth. "We can always reconsider the 'afterward.'"

Willie laughed harshly. "Well, in that case."

"Will Bullethead work with us?" asked Frank.

"Sure. He's always wanted to join, but I pushed him off."

They watched the gunmen as they frisked the passengers to make sure they got the valuables. Lorry started to frisk the woman, and she slapped his face for daring to violate her body. She looked respectable in her dark dress and black bonnet. The gunman laughed, grabbed her, and kissed her. One of the passengers, a husky young cowboy, gritted his teeth and swore. The gunman taunted him, but the cowboy turned away.

Then Bullethead signaled the passengers to get back into the stage, and for the driver to ride. He seemed happy to get away with his skin whole and cracked his whip. The horses pulled and the stage started up, its springs groaning and creaking as it went through the narrow passage between the two cliffs.

The three gunmen watched them ride off, then from his perch on the rocky edge Jess fired a shot in the air. The startled gunmen turned, ready to shoot, but saw Jess Grady holding his hand up, and his two men pointing their rifles.

Bullethead, whose shaved head was the reason for his name, stared up with dark, squinting eyes at Jess Grady. He held himself stiff, bewildered by what Jess might do. He had a heavy respect for the Grady bunch, and he wondered if Jess was planning to pilfer his newly acquired loot.

But Jess was smiling. "Hey, Bullets. No shootin'. Let's palaver."

Bullethead nodded slowly. He could see Frank and Willie but not Jim Hardy, the fast gunslinger. Bullethead decided it would be foolish to fear that Jess would lift his booty. Jess Grady worked the banks and the gold traffic. He told Mike and Lorry to holster their guns. When Jess saw that, he gave the word to ride down.

"What in hell you doin' in these parts, Bullets?" asked Jess curiously. Bullethead worked out of New Mexico.

"We heard about the money shipment to Tucson, and figured, like anyone else, we had a right to ride down and look at it." Bullethead mopped his broad-boned, sweating face. "Then along comes this stagecoach, with easy pickin's. That bank money is gonna be tough. We've heard they got an arsenal guarding the bank. So we took the bird in hand." He grinned.

"Good thinking, Bullets."

Bullethead rubbed the cropped hair of his scalp, and his eyes glittered with the vision of the gold locked in the safe. "Wouldn't surprise me if it was your intention, Jess Grady, to get a very close look at that money. Isn't that what you and your bunch like to do?"

Jess smiled. "Nothing like the sweet smell of money."

Bullethead glanced at Frank and Willie and nodded. "Where you got Jim Hardy stashed? He's got an eye on the bank right now, I'll bet."

Jess looked sad. "I fear we've lost Jim Hardy."

Bullethead looked startled. "Lost Hardy? How?"

"I hear he's been shot."

"In the back? They always hit the best gunmen that way. That's the way they did Bill Hickok."

"No. I heard he got beat in a draw."

A slow smile spread on Bullethead's broad face. "You tellin' me that greased-lightnin' Hardy got beat? Well, well." And he rubbed his hands, as if with pleasure. "And who did it?"

"Man called Slocum."

Lorry grunted. They looked at him. "I knew a Slocum during the war. Marched with the Georgia Regulars, under Pickens. The fella was a wonder with a rifle.

Could shoot out the eye of a rattler from a hundred yards. Could be the same fella."

"Dunno," said Jess. "We're gonna take care of him. After we do the job."

Bullethead stroked his chin, then looked at Willie and Frank, nodded to them, and his eyes crinkled with the effort of thought. Then he said, "So you're gonna hit the bank, you boys, without Hardy. Takin' a chance, ain't you?"

"Tell you the truth," said Jess. "We've done jobs with three men before."

Bullethead grinned. "But this is the bank of Tucson. You must be funning, Jess. They've got a lot of guns watchin' the money."

Jess waited for Bullethead to make his move, and he made it. "I know you got a smart head for bank jobs, Jess. But you ain't got the guns for this one. We'll come into your bunch—for an even split. How about it?"

Jess grinned. "Tell you the truth, Bullets, I been hopin' you'd say that."

At night the stars glittered big and bright in the dark sky as Slocum and Dustin strolled through the streets of the town toward the hotel. By this time most of the saloon drinkers, either sleepy or drunk, were headed for home. Slocum glanced in the window of Lucy's Cafe. It looked empty. They walked on in silence, passing the livery and then the bank, which seemed impregnable, with its solid oak doors shut tight.

"No hurry about the Larrimore Ranch." Dustin's face was solemn. He felt curiously uneasy, as if something bad might happen once he reached the ranch. His father had died there, he had been told years ago, from a surprise Apache attack at night. But if that was so, why had his mother told him to go back and solve the mystery of his father's death? She had not told him till the end because she thought he might leave her. But, dying, she felt it time to square accounts. She hadn't lived long enough to tell him her suspicions. But there had to be something strange about his father's death or she wouldn't have told him to go to Larrimore.

A drunk, singing softly to himself, passed by. He noticed Slocum and grinned ear to ear. "Mister Lightning hisself," he mumbled. Then he staggered to his horse and lifted himself laboriously to his saddle, and sang softly into the night.

Dustin glanced at Slocum sidewise. "Your card game is slow, Slocum, but your gun is fast." His smile widened. "You take a man like Hardy, who never met a gun he couldn't beat. He begins to think himself unbeatable. Everyone who stood up against him goes down. Then he comes up against you. He's still thinking he can't lose. But he loses."

Slocum was silent.

Dustin went on. "What's interesting is that you did Hardy a favor."

"How so?" Slocum's face was grim.

Dustin stopped. "Hardy went out believing himself the best. He never knew he had lost. Didn't have time to work on the idea that he was second best." Dustin's smile was almost subtle. "Yessir, Mr. Slocum. You did Jim Hardy a favor by giving him sudden death."

Slocum looked thoughtful as they walked on. "Gunslinging isn't much of a living. There's always a better gun waiting somewhere. And if you make a big rep, like Wild Bill, there are men who will shoot you in the back for the glory."

"In the territories, it's the world we live in, Slocum. We live or die by the gun."

Slocum's smile was grim as they went into the hotel. "Much better to live by it, Dustin."

7

It was early, and the sun blazed orange as it started its
hot climb into the Arizona sky. Slocum and Dustin came
out of the O.K. Hotel and sauntered down the dusty
street past Riley's Saloon and Gambling Hall, past the
dry goods store, past the Tucson Bank, with its two
guards out front. They stopped in front of a big one-
story structure with a huge sign that said: "MIDSUMMER
DANCE TONIGHT—Don't miss it!"

Dustin turned to Slocum. "They take this dance seriously. Must be a gathering of the clans."

"Gotta get the girls to meet the boys," Slocum said.
"Get the birthrate up. Defend us against the Apaches."
He paused to light a cigarillo. "It takes seventeen years

to turn a boy into a fighting man. And less than one minute for an Apache to wipe him out."

"That's why we need the settlers," said Dustin. "This dance might be fun. We could look in. What dy'a think?"

"I reckon Larrimore can wait a day."

Slocum led the way into Lucy's Cafe, where a handful of customers, eating breakfast, turned sharply to look at him. Some had seen his gunwork at the saloon last night. Slocum and Dustin took a table facing the window.

Lucy came over, a slender young woman with dark brown eyes in a finely boned oval face. She had a neatly packaged figure, and Slocum figured she'd be a fine catch for the right cowboy. He glanced at Dustin, who looked impressed.

"And what kind of breakfast will you be having, two big brawny men?" Her voice was soft and pleasant.

Instantly smitten, Dustin spoke up. "I'm hungry enough to eat a horse this mornin', Miss Lucy."

"Sorry, horsemeat is not on the menu today." Her eyes had a comic twinkle.

Dustin grinned. "In that case, make it three eggs and bacon, four biscuits, and lots of coffee."

Lucy turned to Slocum with a small smile. "And you, Mr. Greased Lightning?"

"The same."

She nodded and walked toward the kitchen, where her Chinese cook prepared the meals.

"Word in town gets around fast," Dustin said.

Slocum shrugged and glanced out the window. A wagon was being loaded with supplies in front of the dry goods store, a cowboy walked his Appaloosa up the street, two cattlemen wearing broad-brimmed hats walked on the boardwalk toward the bank.

Slocum turned to see Dustin looking intently at Lucy moving about. "She's a lovely girl, Slocum. Could make the right man very happy."

Slocum grinned. "Well, why don't you go courting? She'll be at the dance tonight. On such an occasion a girl like her will be looking at the prospects."

Lucy brought out plates of eggs and crisp bacon, browned biscuits and butter.

"Looks very tasty," said Dustin, staring into her brown eyes.

She gave him an enigmatic smile and went off.

Slocum forked a mouthful of eggs and bacon.

Lucy brought back two steaming mugs of fresh coffee. She watched them for a moment. "I like to see a hungry man eat. Especially something I cooked myself."

"You did this?" asked Dustin.

"Just said so."

"Are you married, Lucy?" Slocum asked.

"Are you proposing?" She smiled.

He laughed. "Probably would if I was ready. But Dustin here aims to settle down soon. He's got an eye out for a nice-lookin' filly who knows how to bake a cake."

Dustin blushed. "Now cut that out, Slocum."

Lucy's twinkling brown eyes ran over Dustin, his clean-cut face and well-built body. "Not a bad catch for some nice-lookin' filly. You men might enjoy our dance. There'll be fine-looking ladies there."

"Will you be there?" Dustin asked.

"Might be." She smiled and went to another customer.

Dustin lifted his cup and sipped it thoughtfully. "Lots

of fun going on tonight. Okay if we make Larrimore
tomorrow?"

"I'm in no hurry," Slocum said, his eyes out the window. He saw two husky men swing off their horses and
walk toward the bank. The guards in front of the bank
scrutinized them, then went on talking to each other.

"Wouldn't surprise me if Steve Larrimore came to
the dance," Slocum said. "It's the town's social event.
Might be a good place to meet him."

Dustin looked thoughtful. "Wonder how he'll take it?
Seeing me, after all these years."

The moon, a bright globe of silver, hung over Tucson as
if to light the town on this night of the Midsummer
Dance.

Slocum and Dustin, heading for the dance hall, heard
the sounds of music, laughter, and the clink of glasses.

At the door, Lem, a gnarled cowpuncher, was collecting gun holsters and hanging them on hooks against
the wall.

"Let's have the shooters," he said, grinning. "Gotta
keep the peace tonight."

Slocum loosened his gunbelt and passed it over to
Lem. Dustin did likewise. "Gives you a feelin' of being
naked," Dustin grumbled.

It looked like a fine dance, with colored ribbons
hanging from the walls, a fiddler and a piano, and the
pretty girls. In the background were the matrons, nurs-
ing matrimonial hopes for their darlings. Lively cowboys, perked by the presence of the comely maidens,
stomped about with whiskey courage, which they
sneaked from outside the hall. There were older
ranchers too, all seeming to enjoy themselves.

Slocum could see Millie across the big room, her

yellow hair glowing, flashing smiles at the three cowboys who were sparking her.

Sighting Slocum and Dustin, Millie excused herself
from her three admiring cowboys and traipsed across to
the two strangers. Her three cowboys, watching, didn't
like it much.

"Glad you fellas could make it," she said.

"Well," said Dustin, "you told us there'd be pretty
girls, and we weren't going to miss that."

"Go ahead, make me jealous," she said lightly and
turned to Slocum. "I want you to meet someone.
Come." She took their arms and steered them to a
corner where a man was smoking a cigar.

"Dad," she said to him, "this is John Slocum. He's
the one who helped me out of bad trouble. This is my
dad, Dave Walker."

Walker had a craggy face, a strong nose, and gray
eyes, which suddenly glittered. He put out a strong
hand. "Mr. Slocum, I can't thank you enough for that."

"He's a deadeye, Dad. He picked them off from the
side of the canyon, like rabbits."

Walker's face was grim. "Like skunks." He drew a
deep breath. "Can't figure that thing out. They shot Bart
down in cold blood."

"They talked to him. What'd they want?" Slocum
asked.

"They told him to disappear. That all they wanted
was Millie," Walker said. "But Bart was a man. He
wasn't going to let that happen. So they shot him down
like a dog." He hesitated. "Sounds like they had other
things in mind. Like kidnapping."

Slocum was puzzled. "Why? Are you a rich man,
Mr. Walker?"

"Far from it." It was clear that Walker, too, was puz-

zled. He was just the foreman of the Larrimore, far
from rich. What did they hope to get by grabbing Millie? Did they somehow hope to reach Steve Larrimore
through her? Maybe. But who would these men be?

Millie had said she'd never seen them before.
Walker, thinking of it, shook his head in puzzlement.
Whatever it was, he had plenty of reason to be grateful
to this lean, rugged stranger. Again he smiled at him.

Then Millie said, "And this, Dad, is Dustin Larrimore, all grown up."

Walker was startled. *"This?"* He stared hard, and it
seemed to Slocum that he was jolted more than was
called for, but he made a recovery. He put out his hand
and grinned. "Dustin Larrimore. Excuse me, but I'd
never believe it. You were a thin, sawed-off runt. And
here you are, with a full set of muscles."

Dustin laughed. "That's what happens. Must say, the
same thing happened to Millie."

They looked at her womanly figure, with its bountiful breasts. "Not exactly," said Slocum.

"Much better," said Dustin.

They laughed, even Walker, good-naturedly. Then he
rubbed his chin reflectively. "You haven't seen your
uncle?"

"Not yet."

Walker glanced over the throng. "It's gonna jar him.
To see you all growed out, a fine-looking young man."

Then one of the cowboys who had been in the circle
around Millie came up. The sullen-faced, stout, thick-
necked man nodded to Walker and Slocum, glanced dis-
dainfully at Dustin, then said, "Millie, you're not
dancin'. And they're using up the music. You promised
me this dance."

"That's right, I did, Hank," she said apologetically.

"This is Dustin, a friend of long ago. Hank Mosely."

Mosely had sneaked a couple of drinks, and his face was flushed. And it was plain he didn't care much for Dustin, whom he saw as an upstart rival. "Well," he drawled, "Dustin might be your friend of long ago, but I'm your friend of right now. So let's just dust him off. I've come to collect the dance you owe me."

Dustin stared. "Don't think much of your manners, Mosely. And I'd suggest you mosey along without Millie. She couldn't have the bad taste to dance with someone like you."

"Just a minute," said Millie, both pleased and displeased that the men seemed ready to do battle over her.

Mosely glared at Dustin. "And I don't like your looks, and don't like *you* much, either."

Dustin glowered. "I return the compliment, in spades."

They bristled at each other like fighting cocks, and Slocum and Walker couldn't help but grin.

"Perhaps you'd like to step outside, where we can settle this," Mosely said.

"I'd like that," said Dustin. Millie glanced pleadingly at her father. Walker grinned at Slocum; he didn't mind a bit of fighting at a dance—it livened up things. But he'd try and keep the peace. So he spoke in a stern voice. "Listen, you boys. We came for dancing, not fighting. Don't want that nonsense. You can both dance with Millie. Flip a coin; the winner dances first. How about that? Mosely? Larrimore?"

At the name, Mosely turned sharply to Dustin, and his lip sneered. "So you're a Larrimore. Snooty. Doesn't surprise me. You Larrimores think you own the earth."

Dustin's eyes glittered. "Just walk on, rooster.

You're liable to find yourself flat on the earth."

Mosely, who had a short fuse, turned white and swung a hard right. It caught Dustin on the cheekbone, and he staggered back into Slocum's arms. Dustin gritted his teeth with rage; he plunged forward swinging his fists, connecting with Mosely's cheek and jaw. Mosely was jarred, but he was built stout and strong. He shook himself, then waded in. For the next few minutes there was a whirlwind of hard, swinging fists, bruising blows, and grunts of pain.

"Stop them!" Millie yelled.

Only then did Slocum and Walker, who'd been watching the fight with enjoyment, interfere. Each of them grabbed a fighter, holding his arms, so that he couldn't move. The battlers had had enough anyway, for their faces looked red and bruised.

"What the hell are you fellas fighting about?" Slocum asked.

They rubbed their faces and looked around, embarrassed. The fiddler had not stopped his playing, but the dancers had stopped and were staring at them.

Lem came over. "Are we gonna have to pitch you fellas out?"

Walker smiled. "It's over, Lem. I'm sure they'll behave from now on."

"It's over for *now*," said Mosely, scowling. And he moved to his friend, who had been watching.

"Let me know when you'd like to pick it up," said Dustin grimly.

Millie shook her head. "I can't believe my eyes. And I did promise Hank Mosely this dance." She looked apologetically at Dustin. "Listen, I'll be back. Gotta make peace with him."

Walker laughed. "Mosely's a fightin' cock, and his

dad's got a big spread. The Moselys don't care much for the Larrimores." Dustin watched Millie go across to Mosely. "Can't see what she sees in that ornery cowboy."

"Millie's got lots of beaus, Dustin. She ain't the scrawny little tomboy who used to knock you about in the old days."

Dustin watched them through narrowed eyes. To his surprise, Millie pulled Mosely onto the dance floor. She moved light as a feather and danced gracefully. He held her slender waist tightly, talking, jerking his head at Dustin.

Slocum, who had been amused at the spectacle of two fighting cocks, now looked at his glass of punch. "It needs a charge."

Walker shook his head regretfully. "They're watchin' the punch close, don't want it spiked, trying to keep the dance from gettin' rowdy. Only place to get a drink is outside, back of the hall. What some of the boys are doin'."

Dustin rubbed his reddened cheek. "Think I'll clean up."

Slocum looked after him; he was going outside for a couple of drinks. Slocum watched the dancers and wondered what Mosely had against the Larrimores.

Then Slocum wondered if Jess Grady would make an appearance in Tucson, and if so, when and where. Grady was a man who didn't let up. Like Hardy, he was an unforgiving man who went all the way with his hates. Only he was more dangerous. As the boss of a bunch, he'd be shrewd, secretive, foxy. It wasn't the first time Slocum had run into men like Grady.

And Grady was out to get Dustin—Slocum felt that in his bones. It just couldn't be losing in a poker game, it had to be something else. But what? And what would Grady do? He'd try to hit unexpectedly, Slocum thought.

His eyes roved about. A man was supposed to check his hardware, but if he wanted to, he could hide a weapon. These men looked all right, though—cowpunchers, ranchmen, settlers.

Then Slocum looked toward the door, where two people who had just come in were causing a small commotion.

8

The two people who had just come in were a husky, square-jawed man and a red-haired woman with a commanding presence. Slocum recognized the man—it was Steve Larrimore.

Larrimore spoke playfully to several people and worked his way with the lady through the crowd to the punchbowl. When he tasted the punch he made a face, and the woman with him laughed. By this time he had noticed Walker in the far corner, but he seemed surprised to see Slocum. He spoke to the lady, and she casually followed him.

"I see you've met Slocum," Larrimore said to Walker.

"Millie met him first," Walker said. "He's the one

who pulled Millie out of that bad trouble I told you about."

Larrimore's eyebrows went up. "Slocum. So it was you. We owe you plenty, mister. Millie is the favorite girl in these parts." He looked thoughtful. "You get around a lot, Slocum."

Then he turned to the red-haired woman, who had been observing Slocum with interest. "This is Mona West."

Slocum thought her one hell of a looker, with violet eyes dramatic against her very light skin. She had a pretty mouth, but it seemed tight to Slocum, as if she bottled up her feelings. She had a full figure and plenty of bosom and hip. Slocum could understand Larrimore's interest in her. "I asked Slocum to join us at the ranch, Mona. He's got a fast hand with a gun."

Mona smiled. "It's always good to have the fast gun on your side, Steve. I think he'd fit nicely." Her voice had a honeyed softness, and her eyes gleamed.

Larrimore was smiling. "Better yet, he seems to be in the right place at the right time. That's a very special gift."

Larrimore was not married, Slocum remembered, but Mona talked like the boss's lady.

Walker was listening hard.

"Let me think about it," Slocum said. "I appreciate the offer."

"Anytime," Larrimore said.

Outside, Dustin walked behind the dance hall, where, set discreetly back in a pool of light, surrounded by the shadow of the nearby houses, a heavy man in a big denim coat was standing near his wagon. It was loaded with several whiskey jugs.

Two cowboys in their dance hall finery were pulling from a jug, in turn. One of them, a blond-haired man, wiped his mouth and looked at Dustin. "Hell of a dance, where you can't get a shot of whiskey."

"Not much fun without it," said the other cowboy.

"That's why I'm here, boys," said the heavyset man. "Quarter a drink," he said to Dustin.

"That's robbery, Hiram," said the blond cowboy.

"Listen boy, you're getting personal attention. Ain't I bringing the whiskey to you? You ain't travelin' for it. That's worth something."

"Worth it to me," said Dustin. "Lemme have one." He lifted the jug and drank.

Suddenly the jug blew apart in his hands, the liquor spilling, narrowly missing his body. He heard the bark of the gun and ducked. The second shot seemed to come from the shadows of a building fifty feet away. Dustin, flat on the ground, had no gun, but Hiram did. Hiram was startled by the gunfire and bent low behind his wagon.

"Either shoot or gimme your gun," Dustin hissed. Hiram pulled his pistol and stared into the dark. There was nothing to shoot at. After a few minutes they heard the sound of a galloping horse.

Dustin grabbed the gun from Hiram's hand and ran forward, but the horse, galloping in the shadows with its rider bent low, turned behind a building. Dustin never did get a clear view to shoot.

He returned the gun to Hiram. "What the hell was that?" Dustin asked.

"Who the hell knows," Hiram said. "One of those crazies. Reckon he's got somethin' against drinkin'."

"Or somethin' against me," Dustin said.

"Who'd shoot like that, in the dark, at a man?" asked the blond cowboy.

"A rattlesnake," said Dustin. He picked up another jug and took a long pull.

"That rattlesnake cost me a jug," growled Hiram.

"Lucky he just hit the jug," said Dustin. He gave Hiram a dollar. "Maybe that jug saved my life," he said.

Dustin came through the door, feeling good because of the whiskey and sour because of the shooting. He looked at the dance floor and saw Millie dancing with another of her sparks. He walked toward Slocum, then saw Larrimore. It startled him, as if the sight had stirred curious memories. When he reached the group, Larrimore glanced at him, puzzled.

Walker spoke. "Yes, Mr. Larrimore, it's the boy, Dustin. He's a man now."

Larrimore stared hard, and to Slocum it seemed he was looking at something that had happened long ago. He was transfixed.

Mona, who was also watching Larrimore, frowned. "Steve." Her voice was sharp.

It brought him back to the present, and his poise returned. "Dustin, you look so like your father, I thought you were his ghost." He reached out and grabbed Dustin's hand. "I'm glad to see you."

"Me too, Uncle Steve." Dustin's brown eyes burned as they looked at his uncle.

Slocum, seeing them together, could find little family resemblance. Dustin had a handsome, well-shaped face, with alert brown eyes, and he was built sinewy. Steve Larrimore had rugged, uneven features, gray eyes, and a bulky frame. Different family strains, Slocum figured.

"You're not just passin' through, Dustin? You aim to stop at the ranch?" Larrimore said.

"Like to, if I'm welcome."

"What kind of a remark is that? The place once belonged to your father." Larrimore shook his head. "I'll never understand why Sarah did what she did. Run off with you that night. A very strong lady." He pulled out a cigar. "Didn't know where you landed for years afterward. How is your mother?"

"She died last week," Dustin said.

There was silence. Then Larrimore nodded. "I'm sorry. But she made a bad mistake, grabbing you like that and taking you to nowhere. You should have been on the ranch, where you belonged. With me."

Dustin smiled. "Hope you don't mind if my sidekick, Slocum, visits with us."

Larrimore smiled too. "I'm trying to get him there." He puffed his cigar. "How'd you two meet?"

"A gunman back in Lawson hated to lose at cards. Slocum pulled me out of a bad spot."

Larrimore scowled, then laughed. He looked at Slocum. "You put me in debt, mister. You're welcome to stay as long as you like on the ranch."

Slocum smiled and glanced at Mona. She seemed to like the idea but something was eating her.

Larrimore said, "I'm curious. Who was it gave you a bad time in Lawson?"

"Jess Grady," Slocum said.

There was a silence. "Jess? Damn it." He turned to Walker and Mona and shook his head. "Grady can get to trouble quicker'n a buzzard to a carcass." He turned to Dustin. "We use his bunch sometimes against the Hatfield gang of rustlers." Larrimore puffed at his cigar. "We've got big herds, and there are rustlers prowling around, out to pick us off. We've had a lot of trouble trying to nail the Hatfield gang. So Walker got the bright idea to hire out the Grady bunch to stop'em, to wipe'em out. Set a thief to catch a thief. It's an idea that seems to work." He laughed, and Walker and Mona joined in the laughter. Dustin smiled.

But Slocum didn't smile at all.

Then Dustin saw Lucy, the girl from the cafe, who had hit him hard at breakfast, come through the doors. She was wearing a white gown that showed a finely wrought figure. Her dark hair curled around a delicately molded face. Dustin, looking at her, felt again the wound of Cupid's dart. He hurried over to beat a couple of smitten cowboys who had also spotted her.

"Hi, Miss Lucy," Dustin said. "Hope you're ready for a dance."

"Why not?" she said, smiling. "I came expecting to dance."

Dustin took her hand and led her onto the dance floor, grinning at the other two scowling cowboys.

"Lots of competition for the pretty girls," he said.

"Isn't that how it's s'posed to be?" she asked, looking at his bruises.

He frowned and touched his cheek tenderly.

Lucy repressed a smile. "Could I ask about the fight?"

He shrugged. "Oh, I tangled with a clown named Mosely."

Her brown eyes studied him. "Mosely? So you were fighting Mosely over Millie Walker?"

He felt embarrassed, dancing with this lovely girl and telling her that he had been fighting over another girl. "It wasn't Millie. More like he didn't like the Larrimores."

"Oh, then you didn't fight over a woman. I'm sorry to hear that."

She smiled. "Nothing a woman admires more than a man who'll fight for her."

Dustin gazed into her soft brown eyes and felt himself drowning. "The truth is, Miss Lucy, I knew Millie long ago, as a kid. I feel very friendly about her. I reckon Mosely got jealous."

"Oh", she said.

He cleared his throat nervously. "If it came down to it, reckon I'd fight for the lady, like any red-blooded man."

Lucy gazed at him with the mystery of woman. "I'm glad to hear it." Again she seemed to repress a smile, and squeezed his hand as they danced.

Dustin tingled with pleasure. He looked at her delicate, oval face, thought she looked like a storybook princess, and felt himself in love.

They started another piece of music, this one slow and romantic, and she seemed to want to go on with the dancing, which pleased him. He glanced around and was astonished to see Slocum dancing with Mona

Slocum, holding Mona's slender waist, couldn't help being aware of her female curves. She wore a dress that revealed the deep cleavage of her silky breasts. At times, during the dance, she seemed to stumble against him, and he felt their fullness.

She looked at him provocatively. "You've been invited to join the Larrimore. I hope you do."

Slocum raised his eyebrows. He found Mona one sexy lady, and when her body touched his, it ignited his groin.

"Larrimore seems to have plenty of men," he said.

"It's not the quantity of men but the quality. It's the fast gun that Larrimore needs. The herds are enormous and spread over miles of land. The rustlers keep picking."

He glanced to the far corner, where Steve Larrimore, who rarely looked at the dancers, was talking to Walker and another man.

"And that's why Larrimore hires buzzards like the Grady bunch?" Slocum said.

Mona's eyes were veiled. "It's because of the Hatfield gang. Jess Grady and his boys did a good job of cutting them down. No cause to be sorry about hiring Jess Grady."

"If you touch pitch, Miss Mona, you get dirty."

"Nothing wrong with the Grady bunch," she said. "They haven't busted the laws in this territory."

"That you know of. Dustin and me had a run-in with them, as I told you."

"Yes, but you didn't tell what happened."

"It was Jim Hardy. He was the one."

Her glance was sharp. "You had a mix-up with Hardy?"

He nodded.

Her eyes were wide. "You didn't say what happened."

"I'm here. And he's not."

"You beat him in a draw? Did you?"

He just looked at her.

A strange expression flitted over her face. "So you beat Jim Hardy. The fast gun. Who are you, Billy the Kid? More than ever, you ought to be on Larrimore's payroll. He's very generous with men like you."

Slocum smiled. "I don't hire as a gunslinger."

She hesitated, then suddenly, as if she stumbled,

brought her full breasts against his body. It was a sizzling moment.

She looked meaningfully into his eyes. "What would it take to hire you, other than money?"

Slocum thought for a moment. "What do *you* do at Larrimore?"

"If you're asking do I belong to Larrimore, let me tell you straight. I belong to myself. I'm a free woman who follows her heart and mind. Mr. Larrimore pays me for my work. I supervise the business side of the ranch. And that's the side that needs protecting guns."

She looked toward Larrimore, then back to Slocum. "You breed cattle, feed them, nourish them, brand them, and you're ready to market them. Then someone comes along to steal them."

"You seem to speak for him."

"In business, yes." Her eyes glowed. "Whatever you want, I'm sure you can get it."

He looked at her full breasts, her womanly figure. "Must admit you make an irresistible appeal, Mona. Fact is, I wouldn't mind helping Dustin, if he decides to stay at the ranch."

Mona's face was enigmatic. "How much do you want, Slocum? I told you, you could get it."

"Maybe you're a mind reader, Mona?"

The music had stopped and the dance was ended. He brought her to the side, thanked her for the dance, and walked toward the door to get a breath of air. That Mona left him horny as a stallion.

Slocum looked out the window of his hotel room, at a big moon in a deep blue sky. Its silver light glinted on the great towering canyon. Compared to this timeless stone, man and his tiny wooden huts looked like quick passengers on the planet earth.

Slocum then looked down the dusty street, touched by moonbeams. The dance still yielded up a few night-hawks, having too good a time to go home.

Slocum yawned and lay on the bed. It had been a heavy day, and he was ready for a good night's sleep. Lying there, he couldn't help thinking of Mona. One sexy lady, with her curves in the right places. She had denied any entanglement with Larrimore. It seemed strange but could be true. There was something puzzling about her, but he couldn't pinpoint it.

Then, outside his room, he heard a step, soft, light-weight, and, pulling his gun, he moved soundlessly to the door.

There was no sudden break-in, just quiet scratching on the wood. He opened the door carefully and was jolted at the sight. For discretion she had covered her red hair with a kerchief, and her cloak was drawn up to partly cover her face.

He swung the door wider and she came in noise-lessly, her violet eyes glinting. "Surprised to see me, Slocum?"

"Delighted is more like it."

She pulled off her cloak and the kerchief, and her female presence transformed the room. "I think you're surprised, anyway," she said.

He smiled, because actually he was. Earlier, she had been tossing hints, but he found it hard to believe she'd come here.

"I told you that if you joined Larrimore, you'd get anything you wanted."

"Are you trying to buy me, Mona?" He was smiling.

"No, you can't be bought. Let's say I'm pleasing

myself. You're an attractive man." She looked at the whiskey on the table.

He poured drinks, handed her a glass, and looked at her cleavage. A sexy woman, he was thinking. He had stumbled onto something good.

She sipped her glass. "Where are you from, Slocum?"

"Calhoun County, Georgia."

"Then you fought on the right side."

"The side you fight on is always the right side," Slocum said.

She looked at her drink. "I'm glad that you're on Larrimore's side now, Slocum. I never expected Jim Hardy to go down. Never." She smiled. "Perhaps if you knew how many men his gun has finished off, you might have avoided him."

From his seat, he could see the moon through the window. He raised his glass. "You don't avoid the Hardys of this world. They've got something to prove —and keep trying to prove it."

"Prove? What do they have to prove?"

"That they're the best."

"Is that it? That's all there is?"

Slocum grinned. "It's a lot. I been thinking about it. The draw, it's a game, just like bronco-busting, like poker." He smiled. "You're in a game to prove you're the best. Only thing, the stakes are different. In the draw, you're betting your life."

She sipped her drink. "Men like games like that. They like games that wipe out the other guy. Women are different. They care."

Slocum grinned, looking at her sensual body. "Women play more interesting games." He stepped toward her, and her face lifted. She had a long lower lip, very full, very kissable. He put his lips on her, felt their softness. He slipped his arms round her waist, and she moved close. Her body was warm and lush. He slipped his hand into her dress and felt her velvety skin, her firm, rounded breasts. He felt the nipples. They were erect. His hands caressed her body, her buttocks.

"Get out of your things," he muttered.

She had a voluptuous figure, with silky skin, full hips, and fine thighs. His flesh mobilized. She looked at him with glittering eyes and slipped onto the bed. He followed her. She pleasured in his body, and he enjoyed watching her.

"You're made to give a woman much pleasure," she murmured. Her excitement was at a pitch when he entered her. He held her tight, feeling her depths as she picked up his rhythm. They moved together for a long time, then he felt her body tighten and she groaned softly. He felt the surging excitement, and his moves became dynamic until the climax.

"That was wonderful." Her voice was husky.

Later, just as she was leaving, she leaned down and kissed his cheek lightly. "Look forward to seeing you at the ranch," she whispered. She shut the door softly behind her.

That night he slept very well.

9

Next morning, after bacon and eggs at Lucy's Cafe, Slocum and Dustin were sipping coffee and discussing the dance. Slocum, looking out the window at the sun-bright street, could see two cowboys bringing their horses to the livery, a man loading seed from the general store into his wagon, two customers walking into the bank.

Slocum turned to Dustin, who was toying with a biscuit. "How'd you like your uncle Larrimore?"

"Mighty generous," Dustin said. "He thought my mother made a mistake. Wouldn't be surprised if he was right. What the hell—we had a rough time. Things could have been easier if she'd stayed at the ranch."

Slocum shrugged. "She musta felt it mighty important to get away."

Dustin nodded slowly. "Women get all balled up when they have small fry."

Slocum sipped his coffee.

Dustin grinned. "That Mona is some looker. What d'ya make of her?"

"Talks like she's the lady of the place."

"Might be," Dustin said. "What d'ya think of her?"

"I think she's a barrel of snakes," Slocum said. "Sexy as a rabbit and smart as a fox."

Dustin laughed. "She likes the idea of you working for the Larrimore." He looked sly. "Was it the gun in your holster? Or the other one."

Slocum shook his head. "You got a dirty mind."

Dustin took a biscuit, buttered it, and bit into it. He enjoyed it. Then he frowned. "What gets me is that Larrimore uses the Jess Grady bunch. It's a smart idea. Turning one bad bunch against the other, the Gradys against the Hatfields. But Jess Grady is one mean hombre. You didn't seem to find it funny."

"No. Just to remind you, Grady liked the idea for his gunslinger, Jim Hardy, to steal your winning pot. And cut you down too."

Dustin looked thoughtful, then frowned. "But Grady didn't know that I was kin to Larrimore."

"Didn't know. Maybe didn't care." Slocum lifted his coffee cup. "Or he did know and didn't care."

Dustin scowled and ate the rest of his biscuit. "You figure he's comin' after us?"

"I figure he's going to go where he wants to."

Dustin looked serious. "I meant to tell you last night. But all that dancin'. When I went outside, I was drinking out of a jug. Someone shot it right outa my hands. Whiskey almost spilled over me."

Slocum looked at him.

Dustin shrugged. "Couldn't figure it. Someone didn't want drinkin' at the dance awful bad."

"Did they shoot at any other jugs?"

"No. Just mine."

Slocum looked grim. "Then what happened?"

"It was dark. Man on a horse, got away in the shadows. How do you figure it?"

"I figure Jess Brady had a man in town taking a pot-shot at you."

They were silent.

Slocum lit a cigar, glanced out the window, and saw the back of a well-dressed man in a Prince Albert frock coat go into the bank. There was something about the man. He might have seen him before, but where? Texas? Kansas was it?

He couldn't connect the memory.

Albert Barnes, banker, a florid, heavyset man, was sitting at his desk in the back of his bank, looking at a column of figures. He had just lit a cigar when a well-dressed, broad-shouldered man came toward him with a smile.

Barnes looked up. The man was a stranger, wore a Prince Albert frock coat, a broad-brimmed Stetson, and well-fitted trousers. Mr. Barnes put him down instantly as a businessman ready to do banking in the booming Arizona Territory.

"Mr. Barnes?"

"Yes, sir."

"My name is James Travis. I'm in business in Kansas City. I'm considering a business proposition in this town." He paused. Since I expect to do plenty of banking here, I'd like to inquire about the safety of my deposits." His smile was careful. "I'm informed this is one of the strongest banks in the Arizona Territory."

Barnes took a measure of the man and liked what he saw. "Have a seat, Mr. Travis. I assure you that your money will be safe in this bank. We get the big deposits from cattlemen and shop owners. And I'm happy to tell you this bank had never been cracked by outlaws. Some few have tried." He shook his head. "Those polecats are resting quietly up on Boot Hill."

Travis looked pleased. "I'm glad to hear that. In Kansas City bank robbers have become very bold. It's nice to hear you use strong measures."

"Strong measures—I believe in that. A show of force discourages theft, Mr. Travis. We have five cool-headed guards, each a picked man and deadly with a gun." Barnes leaned back and puffed on his cigar. "I can't see any gang of thugs coming up against them."

Travis looked at the two husky guards who were watching three customers lined up in front of the teller. Two cowboys in denim were writing out deposit slips on the table next to the wall.

"Five guards?" said Travis. "But I see only four. Two out front and two here."

Barnes smiled. "We have another. That's our secret. We have a secret gun." His glance slipped to the wall opposite the safe. Travis, following the glance, studied the wall and noted the small knothole at eye level. A hidden man could easily survey the safe; they had built a special wall, a camouflage. Damned clever, this Barnes, thought Travis. No wonder so many holdup men got chopped down in Tucson. When they got to the safe and were digging for the money, the hidden guard, from that knothole, would pour hot lead into them.

Travis took a deep breath. "I think I see, Mr. Barnes. You have an ace in the hole. Am I right?"

Barnes just smiled broadly and rubbed his hands. "In business and in gambling, Mr. Travis, it's always smart to have an ace in the hole."

Travis grinned. "I understand. I reckon you know how to run a bank, Mr. Barnes. And I reckon I'm ready to do business. If you'll look down here."

Surprised, Barnes glanced down and saw the Colt .44 held in Travis's lap pointed up at him. It came from the slit innner pocket of the frock coat. And from its position it could not be seen by the guards. Travis coughed gently, which made the two cowboys making out deposit slips turn to glance at him.

Barnes paled, and his lips tightened.

Travis spoke in a low voice. "Now, Barnes, don't do anything foolish. It's only money, not worth your life."

Barnes ground his teeth. "Who the hell are you?"

"The name is Jess Grady, and do what I tell you. Call one guard to tell the man behind that wall that you want to talk to him. One wrong move and you're dead."

Barnes bit his lip in fury, but he felt that, whatever he did, Grady couldn't get away with it. Nobody ever had.

"Are you pulling this yourself, Grady?"

"I ain't that dumb. My men are all around. Now do as I say. We don't want to spill your precious blood."

Just then one of the husky guards, a man named John Wilson, glanced at Barnes talking to the stranger who looked like a businessman. Wilson couldn't help notice the man's strong body and rugged face. Wilson walked over. His approach made Barnes tense.

"Everything all right, sir?"

"All right, John," Barnes said, his voice steady, aware

of the hidden gun. "This is Mr. Travis, who is going to bank here."

Wilson nodded pleasantly. "Anything you want, Mr. Barnes?"

Barnes looked thoughtful. "Yes, I do. Tell Turner to come out. I'd like to talk to him."

John glanced again without suspicion at the seated stranger, then walked to the wall door and tapped three times. After a long moment, a hidden door in the alcove squeaked opened softly and a lean-faced, sinewy guard came out, looking puzzled.

"Barnes wants you, Turner."

Turner frowned, because it left the safe unguarded. Barnes had always insisted someone be on "safe watch" during banking hours. Barnes had never ordered him out before.

Turner looked sharply at Barnes and was struck by his closeness to the stranger. Then Barnes winked, and that did it. *Holdup!* Turner's hand snaked down to his gun. Jess Grady raised his pistol one inch and shot him in the chest.

The two guards, in shock, jerked at their guns, but the two cowboys who had been making out deposit slips already had their guns in their hands, and they fired, sending the guards hurtling back and down, their wounds pouring blood.

The two guards outside the bank, startled by the muffled gunshots, turned, pulled their guns, and ran crouching toward the bank door. A volley of gunfire from two more loitering cowboys on the other side of the street, near Lucy's Cafe, cut them down. The guards stumbled and fell to the ground. Two young men from the livery ran out with guns blazing; they were cut down by the gunmen. The street was clear. Barnes, looking through the window, cursed. An ambush; Grady had come with a bunch.

"Stay easy, just go up against the wall," Grady said coolly to the frightened bank customers. "You won't get hurt." Pale and staring, they backed against the wall. None wore guns.

"Open the safe. You've only got seconds," hissed Grady to Barnes, his eyes gleaming death.

Barnes reached down and with a few practiced moves opened the safe.

The two "cowboys," who were Mike and Lorry, came forward, pulled folded bags from under their denim jackets, reached into the safe, and stuffed money and gold into the bags.

Grady glared at the sweating men against the wall. "Don't move or you're dead," he warned. He edged Barnes forward, standing behind him, holding a gun to his body. Then, with narrowed eyes, Grady said to Mike and Lorry, "Move out front. Let's go." He pushed Barnes to the door.

With Barnes behind the two men, they went into the street, holding guns and booty. They started for the horses. The two men outside, Frank and Bullethead, already in the saddle, both holding guns, watched the street. It was empty, except for the dead guards and wounded cowboys.

When the shooting started, a couple of minutes earlier, Slocum, in Lucy's Cafe, had pulled his gun and looked out the window. He saw the two loitering "cowboys" fire at the guards, killing them. Slocum moved fast to the doorway and peered out. The gunmen fired at the cafe doorway, their bullets splintering the wood just over Slocum's head, forcing him back.

Peering out again, Slocum saw the bank door open and the robbers come through carrying money bags and guns. A bulky robber in a frock coat held the banker as a hostage, with a gun to his head. Surprised, Slocum recognized Jess Grady. Cleverly, he was using Barnes and two gunmen as a shield for his body.

One gunman started to force Barnes in to the saddle of a horse.

It gave Slocum his moment, and he fired twice, hitting two gunmen; they catapulted back and fell, one dropping his money bag. The gunmen on horseback fired a fusillade and the bullets shattered the doorway, but Slocum had already slipped back to safety.

Leaving Barnes standing, the gunmen on horseback fired at the restaurant, raced east, and within minutes they had rounded the street, safe from bullets.

With Jess Grady leading the way, the four gunmen raced their horses through a parched landscape, climbing into high rocky land. They kept riding until finally Jess signaled a stop, pulling up near a thicket of shrubs.

When they dismounted, Bullethead pulled a bottle of whiskey from his saddlebag and took a long pull. He passed the bottle to Frank.

Jess lighted a cigar and glanced at Frank and Willie, his boys. They'd come through all right. He was thinking that he had protected them from gunfire by keeping Mike and Lorry out front. Bullethead had lost his men in the shooting. Two less to share the loot, Grady thought with satisfaction. Willie was going to wipe them out anyway, and that gunslinger did it for them.

Grady hadn't been able to see who did the fancy shooting from the cafe. The gunslinger had snapped off two shots, knocking Mike and Lorry on their ass.

"Who was it that did the shootin' from the cafe?" Grady asked. There was silence while they thought of the deadly fire.

Bullethead growled. "That sonofabitch cut down Mike and Lorry like he was shootin' lightnin'."

Willie didn't seem terribly upset by their deaths. "Your boys didn't duck too good." His scarred face, with its broken nose, almost grinned. "That gunslinger looked familiar, though I wasn't waitin' to look."

"It was Slocum," said Frank Baker quietly.

Grady took a deep breath. "Yeah, that's who it was. That damned coyote. We gotta nail him, one way or another."

"Slocum, huh?" said Bullethead. "So he's the one who mowed down my boys. I owe him a bullet up his tail."

Jess grinned. "You might do that, Bullets. That coyote gives us no end of grief."

Bullethead said grimly, "We lost a big bag of money. It cuts down the take. That's a lotta grief. Let's look at what we got."

He pulled out his knife and cut into the money bag; the gold and paper money fell out. The men stared with disappointment; considering the blood spilled and the risks, it was a damned small haul.

"The one Mike was carrying, that was the big one," Frank said.

"All the more reason to tear Slocum apart," said Bullethead. His voice was vicious.

Jess was rubbing his chin, looking at the haul. "Well, I'll be damned. They had a fake back inside that safe. The real gold was behind it. I thought at the time it was short space for the money. That damned banker built a false back inside the safe."

Bullethead scowled. "That was one stinking job,

Grady. I lost my boys, and we got nuthin' much to show for it."

"Ain't enough to go around," said Willie, his gray eyes gleaming, turning toward Bullethead.

Bullethead had his gun in his hand. "I was waitin' for you to say that, you sawed-off dog." His face went stony. "Throw your gun."

Everyone froze.

"Wait a minute, Bullets," said Grady. "Don't go off half-cocked. Willie didn't mean anything."

"I know what he meant," Bullets said, turning his gun on Grady. "Throw your guns, everyone, or I'll fill you *all* fulla lead. And you first, Grady."

Grady's mind worked fast. By trading shots, he had figured, Bullets and maybe one of the bunch would go down. It would mean less men to divvy the loot. But now the gun was aimed at him. His hand had been called.

He glanced at Willie and Frank, then pulled his gun. The others, too, pulled their guns.

"Careful," Bullethead said sharply.

They dropped their guns. Bullethead collected them, grinning. "My mom didn't raise her son to be a fool, Willie. That's why I'm still here. I've been reading you for quite a spell." He turned to Grady. "And I didn't like the way you put Mike and Lorry, my boys, on the outside, to take the heat."

Grady shook his head. "It was how the dice fell, Bullets. You got a suspicious mind."

"Nuthin' wrong with my mind. I'm just trying to figure how to keep you guys off my tail. I know you're thinkin' of comin' after me. And if I was like Willie here, I'd throw bullets in all of you so I wouldn't have to worry about it." He paused, studying them. "But I ain't that kind of a killer."

He reached down to the money bag. "I'm takin' this stuff. I've lost my men, and it's right that I have it. Face around."

He walked to his horse. "I'm going to warn you about tailin' me. It won't be smart. Meanwhile, Grady, I'll give you this. Slocum, who knocked out Mike and Lorry, is gotta pay. I'm goin' to hunt him down. Just a matter of time."

Grady looked over his shoulder. "Hey, Bullets. There'll be a posse comin'. And we've got no guns."

"I know that." Bullethead grinned, but he waited.

"After they go through us, Bullets, they'll keep comin' after you."

Bullets sighed. He was aware of that. "So what? I ain't going to give you guns to mow me down."

Grady nodded. "Makes sense. But I'll give you my word. We call a truce. It was a bad job. You lost your boys. I feel I owe you something."

Bullets considered. "I believe you, Jess. But I'm not taking chances. I'll do this for you. Follow my trail, *slow,* for half a mile. The guns will be at the foot of a tree. When you get the guns, move off my trail. I'll know if you don't. Do we have a deal?"

"We've got one, Bullets."

Bullethead swung over the saddle, and the men turned sideways to watch him.

His gray eyes glittered. "No bad moves, Grady. Ain't worth it."

He hit the flank of his horse, and it leaped forward as he rode east.

Slocum, followed by Dustin, walked from Lucy's Cafe to the front of the bank, where the two robbers lay sprawled. Barnes had pounced on the money bag, dropped by the dead robber. He looked into it and smiled. When a teller ran from the bank, Barnes called to him. "Tim, take this bag and put it back in the safe."

Then he walked to stand alongside Slocum, who was looking down at the robber. One was dead, the blood spattered over his chest, as if it exploded. The other looked far gone, his face pale, his eyes half shut. The bullet had pierced his side, and blood soaked his shirt and jeans.

He looked at Slocum standing over him. "You son'o'bitch," he muttered.

"Robbing banks isn't an easy profession," Slocum said. He stared up the street at the two wounded cowboys and the two dead guards.

"You're lucky to be dying quick. You'd be hanging instead."

"Go to hell."

"Ought to hang him anyway," Dustin said grimly, looking at the dead guards.

"Too bad he's dying so quick," Barnes growled.

Men had come out from the nearby shops and livery and were gathering around the fallen cowboys and the guards.

Slocum bent down. "Who was running your show?"

"Who?" The robber muttered, and he looked up with a painful grin. "Just wait. Bullethead Moran will find you. He'll hunt you down for this. You're a goner, Mister."

Barnes scowled at him. "You look like the goner to

me." He turned to Slocum. "Man inside told me his name was Jess Grady."

Slocum nodded. "That's the hombre. It was his bunch."

Barnes looked grim. "We'll send a posse. Most of what they took was in the bag they dropped. And they didn't get much." He lowered his voice. "I've got a secret partition in my safe, and those buzzards never got to the real money."

Slocum nodded. "That's good. It'll make them mean with each other."

Barnes looked at the dead guards on the street. He shook his head. "A bad day." He turned to Slocum. "You've got a quick gun. You saved my skin, mister. And saved the bank's money. I hope there's something I can do for you. I'll put up reward money."

Slocum shrugged. "Did what a man should do."

Dustin stared at him, then turned to Barnes. "Be nice if he gets the reward. He needs the money—he plays lousy poker."

Slocum looked down at the robber. His eyes were open, staring and fixed. While they had been talking he had died.

"Who the hell is this Bullethead?" he asked Barnes. "Have you heard of him?"

"A small-time thief. He robs stages. Never thought he'd tackle a bank. Reckon they heard about the big deposit and decided to try their luck. Bullethead and Grady and their boys."

"They were six," Dustin said. "They've lost two. Now there's four."

Barnes looked grimly at the dead robber. "This one's dead, but that bunch did a lot of bloodletting. I have two dead and three wounded. And these two cowboys are hurt. We can't let them get away with that." He looked at the men gathering near the livery with their horses and walked over to them.

Slocum rubbed his chin. "They're getting up a posse, Dustin. Reckon we should ride with them."

Dustin shrugged. "I don't know. That bunch was rotten, but I'm aiming for the Larrimore. My mother asked me to find out about my father. That's on my mind."

"I understand. But think about this. Last night, someone tried to potshoot you. And it isn't the first time. It keeps going on, doesn't it? And it's this Grady bunch. Why are they doing it?"

"It may be coincidence. Last night, someone didn't like us drinking and popped the jug. As for the Grady bunch, you said yourself that Grady hates to lose money. And we did knock off some of his boys. He doesn't like that. Matter of revenge."

"We don't really know. Maybe we can find out."

"How do we do that?"

"Grab one of 'em and squeeze it out of him. That's why I think we oughta go with the posse."

Dustin looked grim. He wanted to get to the ranch. He ached to find out about his father and the secrets buried at the Larrimore. But he did understand Slocum's point. If the coyote shooting at him had hit true, then the mystery of his father's death would never be solved. First the bushwhacker, then his father. That was the logic.

"Okay," Dustin said.

They walked toward Barnes and the six-man posse, who were saddling up to ride.

"We'll ride with the men," Slocum said to Barnes.

"That's wonderful. A gun like yours ought to be a big help. This is our lawman, Jim Trumbull. He'll be in charge."

Trumbull, a rugged husky man with high cheekbones and flat blue eyes, stared at Slocum. "Glad to have you along, Slocum. You did fine work here. But I want it understood mister, I'm running the show."

"Sure, Sheriff. We understand that." Slocum smiled and started for his horse.

10

It was midday when the posse climbed the high ground and reached a thicket of shrubs. They pulled up to examine the tracks.

"Looks like one of them pulled away here," Trumbull said.

"Surprises me we don't find a body," said Slocum.

Trumbull looked at him. "Why say that?"

"They didn't get much money. And two men were shot down. They can't have thought it much of a job."

Trumbull's flat blue eyes stared at him. "So you figure they had a showdown here?"

"Not a showdown. One of them pulled his gun on the others, took the loot and rode off."

Trumbull's eyebrows lifted. "Where do you read all that, mister?"

Slocum showed him a couple of prints. "Three guns tossed. Here's the prints."

Trumbull studied the marks. "Them's gun marks, all right. Pretty smart to figure it. But if it's true, we got three unarmed men out there. We'll pick them up fast."

Slocum sighed. "Not too fast. You don't know what's ahead. Now these three men are following one renegade. And they've got to expect a posse. They're not goin' to sit around unarmed and wait for us."

Trumbull's jaw was tight. He was running this posse. And he didn't care for second-guessers. "There are three men out there—without guns. It's the best time to grab them. You've seen the damage they've done with guns."

"That's right. They're hardcases. But I'd go slow."

"Look, Slocum, you and your boy here are free to do what you want. The men with me are deputies and act under my orders. We're going all-out to nail these killers." He looked at his men. "Let's go." He hit the flank of his sorrel and it jumped forward. His men heeled their horses, following close behind. They rode fast on a flat curving trail sided with shrubs, rocks, and an occasional tree.

Dustin shook his head. "Funny how a tin star makes a man suddenly feel ten feet tall."

"Who knows? Trumbull might be right," said Slocum. "And he might be lucky. The bunch don't have guns, and it might be a good time to trip them. But they're hardcases. They've survived pursuit for years. Whatever they're doing, they're dangerous."

Riding with care and at a canter, they followed the posse trail. Slocum, who could read signs like a book, would stop often and study the prints. He used his field glasses to study the terrain up ahead. Once, in the distance, he had a clear view and picked up the posse running fast.

He passed the glasses to Dustin, who studied them and said, "Won't be long now. If the posse corrals those buzzards, I'll turn back. They won't need us."

Slocum said nothing, but kept watching the tracks of the Grady bunch until he lost them behind a rank of broken cliffs. The land was now dense with brush and rocky escarpments.

A south wind came up and blew white dust, but the sun's rays still hit the earth hard. They paused at a waterhole to let the horses drink and to wash the dust off their faces, then started again, following the posse trail.

From the tracks, Slocum noted that Trumbull kept the posse horses running hard.

Once he stopped to examine the ground carefully and looked puzzled. "Something's going on. The Grady bunch were following the renegade. But they've swung away and are heading north."

"Why d'ya suppose they did that, Slocum?"

"Don't know. They had no guns. Only way to get their guns would be to stick on the trail of the renegade until they could bushwhack him. I figured that was their aim."

Dustin stared down at the tracks, then toward the broken cliffs. "But they pulled away. Wonder why."

"Maybe they hope the posse will split up." Slocum looked grim. "Or they don't need to follow the renegade. Not anymore."

"Meaning what? They have guns now?"

Slocum nodded.

Dustin looked at him. "You're not a bad man to have along when there's a war on, Slocum." He grinned.

"Like you'd know what the enemy is thinkin' and how he's movin'."

They mounted up to follow the posse tracks. "We're always in a war out here," Slocum said, "because everyone has weapons. Got to guess right. Guess wrong, you're dead."

Dustin couldn't help smiling to himself. Slocum made him feel secure, as if he could handle most anything. He had an aura of unbeatability. And yet there were plenty of hard-talking, hard-drinking cowboys who had that confident air, that unbeatable aura, who went down. Could happen to Slocum, too. Nobody was unbeatable. Some of the great guns of the West were gunned down; if not by a faster gun, then by a back-shooter, out to win notoriety. Or a posse.

His mind slipped back to the dance, and he thought of Lucy. Something about her had hit him hard, and he felt that if things ever settled down for him, he'd seriously court her. If there was such a thing as love at first sight, this was it.

Then he heard the sound of guns. Muffled sounds, coming from behind the jagged cliffs. The firing was quick, intense. Then there was silence.

Slocum looked at Dustin. "Hell of a lot of gunfire."

"Yeah. A lot of guns."

"That would mean the bunch got guns after all."

"Let's find out."

They raced their horses along a trail thick with wiry shrubs. As they moved closer to the broken cliffs, the brush became dense.

"Good spot for an ambush," Slocum said. "From here on we go careful." They tethered the horses, and Dustin followed Slocum as he moved with quiet craft from one protective spot to another. It was slow going.

Slocum thought about Grady—what he would do, where he'd position himself, if he'd somehow got guns.

Jess Grady always felt he'd make a great general because he knew strategy. He knew the land and how to use it smart. And when it came to analysis of tough spots, his mind worked fast.

Like when Bullethead surprisingly took control by pulling his gun first; Grady had quickly agreed to drop his gun. He didn't argue with a drawn gun, it was stupid. Men holding guns, Grady knew, were always ready, because of an accursed desire to feel powerful, to pull the trigger. So he agreed with Bullets.

And Grady thought fast about the pursuing posse, persuading Bullets to leave their guns at a tree. When Bullets wanted Grady's promise that he wouldn't hunt him down for the money, Grady gave it. When you faced a man's gun, you told him whatever he wanted to hear. Later, when you had your own gun, you could reconsider. Bullethead had taken money that Grady had schemed carefully to steal, risking his skin and that of his men. Did Bullets really believe he'd get away with that?

One thing Grady believed in—you didn't betray your own men, your partners in crime.

Grady therefore firmly intended to blow Bullethead away, but at the right time. What made him hesitate was Bullethead's anger with Slocum for shooting his boys. If Bullets wiped Slocum out, it would be a big burden off Grady's back. He decided to give Bullets time to mow Slocum down. Bullets was a man for hard action, when it came to squaring accounts, getting revenge. He'd go after Slocum fast. And with Slocum out of the way, life would be much easier.

That's how Grady figured it, but after they found their guns at a big tree trunk, Willie Stone threw a monkey wrench. Willie said, "Let's go after that buzzard Bullets and get our money."

"No, Willie, we won't do that."

"But he's got our money, Jess."

"Listen, we've got to worry about the posse. We'll get Bullets later. He's going after Slocum, and Bullets gets his man."

"Don't worry about Slocum," said Willie. "I'll get him. I don't like Bullets spendin' our money. We went through plenty to get it."

Grady stared at the trail behind him, then up ahead to where the land became thick with brush. "Listen, if we don't take care of that posse, nobody here will spend any money."

"That's right, Willie," said Frank Baker quietly.

Willie grimaced and shrugged his shoulders. "Okay. What do we do about that damned posse?"

Grady smiled. "They been riding real hard, like they got nothin' to worry about."

Frank Baker stroked his chin. "Can't figure why they're coming so fast. Not too smart."

"I'll tell you why, Frank," Grady said. "Someone there was smart enough to dope out that we had a falling-out and gave up our guns. Someone can read signs real smart."

They looked at each other.

"What they don't know," Grady said, "is we got the guns back."

Willie grinned. "That should make it short and sweet."

"Yeah," said Grady, his lips twisting with the fun of it. "We'll find a good spot. I can see it from here, 'bout a half mile up ahead. Off the side of those busted cliffs. Lots of places in that thick brush to say hello to that posse."

Trumbull was a lawman who hated desperadoes, but there was one he hated with ever fiber of his body, and that was Willie Stone. Trumbull's younger brother, Tommy, whom he had loved and cherished, had been mowed down in Tombstone by Willie Stone. Trumbull learned about it later. The two had had bad words in the Eldorado Saloon, and that reptile, Willie, went outside, waited behind a building for Tommy to come out, and put a bullet in his back. Trumbull had never forgotten the name Willie Stone.

Later, he discovered that Willie ran in the Grady bunch. He kept an eye open for that bunch, and once, to his amazement, he heard that Steve Larrimore was using them.

Well, he didn't have anything on Jess Grady, but he wanted so much to hang Willie Stone that he dreamed about it. So he rode out to the Larrimore Ranch and asked what the hell was going on, why was Larrimore using a shady pack of gunmen like the Grady bunch?

Larrimore told him it was the one way they had found to stop the Hatfield rustlers who kept grabbing his stock.

Trumbull didn't like that, but said, "Maybe that's okay. But I want Willie Stone. That bastard shot my brother, Tommy, in the back."

Larrimore stared at him. "Then you go ahead and take Willie. Trouble is, I don't know where the Grady bunch is. They work on their own. It's my man Walker who deals with Grady, who pays him. We never see the bunch around here."

That deeply disappointed Trumbull, and for a time he hung around the Larrimore, but he never saw any sign of the Grady bunch. It chewed his guts that Willie Stone was still walking around while his beloved brother was dead.

Until the robbery at the Barnes bank, Trumbull had seen neither hide nor hair of the Grady boys. Now he learned from Barnes that Jess Grady and his men had done the robbery and the killings at the bank.

That had finally put him on the trail of Willie Stone, and now, riding after these polecats, he felt his long hunt would soon be over. Willie Stone was one hard-case, Trumbull promised himself, he would hang on the spot, instant justice.

It made Trumbull jump when he discovered that the Grady boys were riding without guns. He knew they were dangerous men, as Slocum had said, but most lawbreakers were dangerous. And, in his time, he'd hanged plenty.

Already, in his imagination, as he was pushing his horse, he could see Willie Stone dangling from a tree. But he would tell him first what a rotten, back-shooting skunk he was, might even put a bullet or two in his carcass before he hanged him.

These were his thoughts as he led his men, hot on the heels of the running bunch, now without weapons, the best time to grab them.

Trumbull was racing fast on a trail through a thicket

of shrubs, brush, and rocks. The prints were fresh, only minutes old.

And that's when all hell broke loose from behind the brush. The bullets hit from three sides, raining death on the posse. They went down spilling blood.

As Trumbull, with three bullets in his body, lay on the ground, he smelled the musty earth. He thought suddenly of Slocum's warning to go slow, not fast. Trumbull turned painfully to look at his posse. Dead, all of them, their bodies still leaking blood.

He thought of Willie Stone and died with a curse on his lips.

Slocum, gun in hand, crept toward the thicket. He saw the horses first, nibbling at the vegetation. Then he saw the men lying in the distorted positions of dead men. They were riddled with bullets.

Dustin's face was grim as he looked at the bloody bodies.

Slocum moved warily, studying the tracks, putting together what had happened.

"They were ambushed from separate positions, behind brush and rocks. The posse didn't know what hit them."

Dustin looked at Trumbull. His expression, frozen by death, was one of fury and hate. "He went out knowing something," Dustin said. "Maybe knowing what a blasted fool he'd been."

Slocum looked thoughtful. "A killer bunch. They've shot six here, six in town. A bloody day."

Dustin's lips were compressed. "They're deadly. Should we get some backup?"

"It's easy to be deadly against a dumb posse," Slocum said.

"They're ridin' north. Where do you think they're headed?" Dustin asked.

"Looks like Salt Creek." Slocum looked thoughtful. "Let's give them something to think about."

They went back for their horses and began tracking again.

11

Salt Creek was a town for desperadoes. They gathered from the nearby territories, loafed, drank, schemed, fought each other, until, bored, they finally departed. Desperadoes felt safe in this town of decayed huts, abandoned years ago when the mine wore out. No lawman dared show up in Salt Creek.

It was an ideal spot for Jess Grady and his boys to stop and ease up from the strains of their recent exertions. They went to Durk's Saloon, where a number of disreputable characters hung out. They sat at a table, tanked up, each with his own thoughts.

Jess was thinking that a lot of effort had gone into robbing the Tucson Bank, and a lot of blood had gotten spilled, but they didn't have a dime to show for it all.

Bad luck. They'd lost one bag of money, the big one, when Slocum shot Lorry, who was carrying it. Slocum was a bone in Grady's throat, and he prayed Bullethead would take care of him. He expected Bullets would go after Slocum hot and heavy. Bullets would grieve over his boys, Mike and Lorry, who had been with him in Texas for years doing petty holdups.

Jess lifted his glass and drank. Yes, Bullets would want revenge, and the quicker the better.

Then Willie, who'd been drinking hard, spoke up. "Jess, I been thinkin'."

Jess and Frank Baker looked at him.

"That's a risky thing for you to do," said Frank.

Jess laughed and looked with pleasure at Frank. He loved that polecat. Frank Baker was a brick, a golden gun, a smart rider who always used his eyes and brain. He was a sinewy lad, with dark eyes, a square face, and a strong nose and chin. He could track like an Apache, shoot straight, and his guts never failed. Whatever was happening, Jess thought, he could always depend on Frank.

"Listen," said Willie, his voice rising. "I get sick every time I think about Bullets. How he grabbed our money and ran with it." He turned to Grady. "Jess, we made a mistake letting him take it."

"And what about the posse?"

"We could have nailed Bullets, got our money, and blasted the posse anyway. They figured we didn't have guns."

Jess shook his head. "No. They figured that one man took the guns. If we had followed Bullets, they'd figure we got the guns back. Everything would be different."

Willie shrugged it off. "Main thing to consider is he's got the money."

"What're you worrying about?" said Frank.

"I'm worried that he's got the money and we ain't. We spilled a lot of blood just to get nuthin', Frank."

"But Bullets is goin' to come here," said Frank.

Willie stared. "Oh, yeah? What makes you say that?"

"He was goin' east. He'd have to travel thirty miles to get supplies. He ran out yesterday. He'll have to turn and come here."

"That's good." Willie grinned. When Willie grinned, his broken nose and his crooked mouth made him a ferocious sight.

Jess and Frank looked at him, then laughed.

Willie didn't mind their laughing. He liked it, in fact. But if it had been a stranger, he'd have his gun out shooting. "So all we do is wait," he said.

"Yeah, and when he comes, we don't touch him," said Jess.

Willie's mouth tightened. He didn't like it.

Jess sighed. "We want Bullets goin' after Slocum. We need to get rid of that varmint. He keeps spoiling everything."

"I told you, I'll take care of Slocum," Willie said quietly.

Jess stroked his chin, his gray eyes glittering. "Let Bullets do it, Willie. Slocum knocked off Jim Hardy, and Jim was our best. Slocum is greased lightning. And a cagey dog. Why should I risk you? We've lost plenty of our boys. Willie, the trick is to let the other guy stick his neck out to do the job. Back at the bank, I had Mike and Lorry cover you, so when the bullets flew, you didn't get hurt. That was Slocum, too, doin' the shootin'. Remember, in Lawson, we had a setup on the Larrimore kid. Who stepped in to stop it? Slocum, again. He's our jinx. Let Bullets try."

Willie shrugged. "Maybe you know best. There'll be time and tricks enough to take care of Slocum." He lifted his glass and drank. "But if Bullets comes here, perhaps we can persuade him to divvy the money."

Jess smiled. "Now that's a nice idea. He's not dumb. If he's forced to come here, he'll be reasonable about the money."

"Well, speak of the devil," said Frank Baker, whose seat faced the batwing doors of the saloon.

They turned to look. There was Bullethead with his hands at the sides of his powerful body with its barrel chest.

A few men knew him and called a greeting, but his eyes, in his thick, bulletlike head, never left the Grady bunch once he saw them.

Jess smiled.

At that, the look in Bullethead's face changed, and he too smiled and came forward to their table, his body alert.

"Surprised?" asked Willie.

"No, Willie. I saw your horses outside," said Bullets.

"Relax," Jess said.

"Sure," said Bullets, who'd never trust anyone as far as he could kick them, most specially a warthog like Willie. He sat down.

"What brought you here, Bullets?" said Frank, winking at Jess.

"Why not?" said Bullets. "We got a truce. I knew you'd be here."

The bartender, Durk, brought over a glass and a bottle. "Hello, Bullets. Where's your boys?"

A doleful look wrenched Bullethead's broad face. "Lost them, Durk. Lost the dearest friends I had on this earth. Mike and Lorry. Practically my brothers."

"Sorry to hear that," said Durk.

Bullets bit his lip and there was venom in his voice. "If it's the last thing I do, I'll see they get revenge."

Durk nodded and went back to his bar.

Jess watched Bullets warily. When Bullets talked of revenge, he seemed to mean Slocum, but Bullets also knew that his boys had been set up as a screen, in case of gunfire. Bullets had to believe that Jess was almost as guilty as Slocum.

Jess watched Bullets with eagle eyes. "By the way, Bullets. It was a good thing you left us our guns," he said.

"Why was that?"

"The posse came."

Bullets studied him. "They don't seem to have hurt you none."

Willie laughed. "Naw. It was them got hurt. Blasted every mother's son."

Bullets smiled slowly. "Reckon it was nice of me to leave you the guns."

"It was smart, Bullets," Jess said.

"It's also nice to see you, Bullets," Willie said.

"Wonder why?" Bullets filled his glass and drank half of it.

"You didn't play square with us on the money," Willie said.

"I lost my boys."

"That's how the dice fell, Bullets. It wasn't right for you to take it all. We stuck our necks out. Why should we come out empty?"

Bullets looked at Jess. "I thought we had a truce."

Jess smiled. "There is a truce, like I said. We ain't pulling guns. But Willie is tellin' it right. We stuck our necks out, and we should share the take."

Bullets lifted his glass, and the Grady bunch watched him, edgy.

He spoke to Jess. "You still got your men. You can do jobs with them. I got nobody. I'll have to look for new men. And they ain't gonna be as good as Mike and Lorry."

Willie put his finger to his broken nose and twisted it, as if trying to straighten it. "It's the fall of the dice, Bullets. We can't argue with that. You got our money."

Bullets was silent, then laughed. "Willie, I'm going to divvy. But I thought I'd mention that you're the nearest thing to a skunk I ever met."

Willie's black eyes burned, and the air cracked with tension. He looked at Jess, then grinned his ferocious grin. "Bullets, today we're gonna be all right together. Tomorrow don't come in the range of my gun."

Bullethead's smile was vicious. "You pipsqueak. That goes for you, too."

Then Jess said, "Dunno why you men are fightin'. There's money to be made if we fight together. The other way could be Boot Hill. Maybe for both of you."

"That's how I see it," Frank Baker said.

There was heavy silence, and Willie squirmed. "Then let him apologize," said Willie. "He's the one doin' the badmouthin'."

Again a long silence.

Jess spoke. "What about it, Bullets?'

"Okay, I apologize."

Slowly everyone smiled. They leaned forward to pick up their drinks.

"Now about splitting the haul." Bullets pulled a leather pouch from inside his denim jacket. "This is for you three. I took my share."

When they stared at him, he looked boldly at Jess.

"Did you think I'd come here unless I was ready to make the split? Be like askin' for a pine box."

Jess laughed. "Bullets, you're a smart buzzard, and we'd like to have you work with us." He turned to his men and stood up. "Let's take this stuff outside and find a safe place to count it and divvy it up."

"How we know it's an even split?" asked Willie, his eyes small.

Again there was silence.

"I got a rough idea," said Frank Baker. "I looked at it real careful when we opened it." He smiled. "Bullets ain't that dumb. For a few dollars, he ain't gonna fleece his friends."

"No, I ain't that dumb, Frank," said Bullets.

He watched them go out the door and poured himself another drink. He sat there about twenty minutes, thinking. His mood was lousy, because he was remembering his boys and missing them. They'd been together, a tight bunch, for years. And he'd been their leader. But now, if he joined the Grady bunch, Jess would be top dog. He'd have to kowtow. And he hated that skunk Willie, who'd shoot his grandmother for a dollar. He didn't know how long he could work alongside a lowlife like that before they'd have a showdown. And after that, who knew how Jess and Frank would take it.

Bullets began to feel sorry that he'd come to Salt Creek, but there had been no other out. He would have had to ride forty miles to the nearest town, and he might have run into Apaches. He'd given up money that he felt rightfully belonged to him, because Jess Grady had sacrificed Mike and Lorry when they left the bank. Jess was a lowdown buzzard too, he thought.

But most of all it was Slocum. He was the polecat

that had shot down his boys. His was the gun that did the killing. He'd glimpsed Slocum at the door of Lucy's Cafe and fired at him twice, driving him back into the restaurant. The man was slippery, and he had come out for two lightning-quick shots that had knocked Mike down, then Lorry. And Lorry had a heavy money bag. It was rotten luck and a rotten job all the way.

Bullethead's eyes idly moved to the men at the bar, and he felt a jolt, as if he'd been hit by a thunderbolt. There, standing cool as a hunk of ice, holding a whiskey glass, stood the man he'd been thinkin' about. *Slocum. When did he come in?* It seemed an impossible coincidence, and he wondered if his imagination had tricked him—that he wanted that polecat so much, he had turned some lookalike drinking man into Slocum. He shut his eyes tight, then opened them, expecting to see someone else. But no, it was the same man. Could it be? Was it Slocum? After all, he hadn't gotten that much of a look at the gunman at the cafe, since all hell was breaking loose and they were racing their horses to get out of town.

Now the man at the bar was looking at him. Bullets tried to think. Jess said he'd wiped out the posse. Wouldn't Slocum be in the posse? So what the hell was he doin' here? Maybe he hadn't been in the posse, or maybe he had survived the ambush.

What did it matter? Here was the lowlife who had wiped out his beloved sidekicks, and he had to pay. Trouble was, Slocum seemed to have recognized him. Why wouldn't he? Slocum had been near the bank, firing from the cafe doorway. Also, when he and Willie had shot the outside bank guards after loitering near the cafe, Slocum, inside the cafe, must have seen them, especially if he was near the window.

So Slocum had a good idea who he was.

It was showdown time, though not the way Bullets wanted it. He had heard of Slocum's shooting speed. Be stupid to draw against him. Bullets had a derringer in his sleeve, because you never knew. He thought fast. He'd go to the bar, order one, and try to get close to Slocum but keep another man between them. Then reach over easy and shoot the bastard with his derringer. He'd never expect that. He'd be watching if he went for his holster. That was how to do it. And who'd give a damn? Everyone here was an outlaw. Slowly he emptied his glass, shifted it to his right hand, stood up, and started for the bar.

It was Slocum, all right, who had come into Durk's Saloon with Dustin just a short time ago. Slocum had looked at the horses tied to the rail outside the saloon but saw only one that looked as if it had been hard ridden.

"They're not here now," Slocum said to Dustin. "We'll go in. They may have been here, or may come later."

Dustin nodded. He'd been looking at the men in Salt Creek and they looked bad, outlaws and drifters. All running like hell from the law.

They went into the saloon, ordered whiskey from Durk, and Slocum looked for faces he'd seen at the bank shoot-out. He knew what the Grady bunch looked like; he'd seen them in Lawson.

But he'd seen new faces in the bank holdup. He remembered a barrel-chested man, one of two who had shot the outside bank guards. Slocum thought of the wounded holdup man who with his dying breath had viciously told him Bullethead Moran would avenge his death.

And there, clear as daylight, was Bullethead sitting at the table, by himself. His head was shaped like a bullet; he had to be Bullethead. Slocum recognized him. This man had shot the guards while they were running toward the bank, and he had shot at Slocum in the cafe doorway.

Now he had an odd look on his face. He'd been sitting with three men, from the look of the glasses on the table—the rest of the bunch. Where were they?

He watched Bullethead deep in thought, probably figuring his move. Slocum watched him stand, take an empty glass, and shift it to his right hand. Slocum's eyes narrowed. You didn't put a glass in your right hand if you intended to use your gun. But his instinct told him this buzzard had killing on his mind; Slocum had run into too many killers in his time not to pick up the smell.

There were a few beat-up looking men drinking around Slocum; Dustin stood next to him. To Slocum's surprise, Bullethead sauntered directly at him. His eyes were on Slocum, but he seemed easy, as if the last thing on his mind was jerking his gun. He edged to the bar and put his empty on the wood.

"Pour one, Durk."

Bullets was aware that Slocum was watching him real sharp, and, whatever he had had in mind, he suddenly made a shift. "Seen you before, mister?" Bullets said.

"Reckon you have."

Bullets said nothing, just lifted his glass to drink. He didn't seem in a hurry about anything. "What's the handle?"

"Slocum."

"Whatcha doin' in Salt Creek, Slocum?"

Slocum smiled. "Lookin' for a bunch of buzzards who shot some friends."

"Lost some friends, did ya?" Bullets looked grim. "I lost a couple too. My sidekicks. A bad shoot-out." He drank part of his drink. "You sound lucky. They shot your friends but missed you."

Slocum's eyes glinted with humor. "Yeah, I'm lucky. I wouldn't be surprised if you were lucky too."

"What's that mean?"

"Nothing much. Your sidekicks were shot, but you're alive and kicking. That's lucky." Slocum shifted his position. "What's your handle? You didn't say?"

Bullets cleared his throat, and his eyes looked mean. "They call me Bullethead."

Slocum nodded. "Funny thing. This polecat said that someone called Bullethead would pay his death off in blood."

Bullets looked jolted. He swallowed hard. "He said that? When did he say that?'

"Just before he died. He said Bullethead Moran would come and tear me to pieces." Slocum's face was calm, but his green eyes had a steely glitter.

Bullets swallowed hard. It was the most painful thing he could have heard. Mike had died believing he'd be revenged. And Bullets wanted nothing in the world more than to kill this hombre. But the man in front of him had a quicker draw than Jim Hardy, the best Bullets had ever seen. There was no way in a million years he could outdraw Slocum. It'd be instant death.

"I figure you're trying to push me."

"Wouldn't be surprised, Bullets. You shot two men in Tucson. You shot at me. Your bunch bushwhacked five of my friends." His eyes glittered hard. "Your time is up."

The man nearby started to move back.

Bullets didn't like that. His face paled. "I'm not goin' to pull my gun, Slocum. Not on you. You're goin' to have to shoot an unarmed man." He smiled grimly. "And you're not the kind to do that."

There was silence. Nobody moved. Slocum seemed puzzled.

Bullets smiled vindictively. "I'm walkin out. If you shoot, you'll have to shoot me in the back."

With his right hand, his shooting hand, he put his glass on the bar and turned away slightly from Slocum, swinging his left arm.

It brought the derringer down from his sleeve to his hand, and he was bringing it up to fire.

"Look out!" Dustin yelled.

Slocum's gun barked, and Bullethead was flung back against the bar and fell against it. He looked down at his chest; it was gushing blood. Bullets still had the unfired derringer in his hand. His face was white as chalk. He looked up from his chest at Slocum and slowly began to raise his hand to shoot.

Slocum watched.

Everyone in the bar watched.

Bullets strained in agony, his strength gushing out with his heart's blood. He got the derringer two feet off the floor, then his hand fell limply and he fired. Into the floor.

Then he died.

Slocum looked around the saloon. The men here, outlaws and drifters, were interested in the game of death, but nobody cared one way or another who lived or died in Salt Creek. They looked at the dead Bullet-head, then at Slocum, and they felt no desire to mix it up with a smart gun like this one.

Slocum could read it in their eyes.

"Let's go," he said to Dustin.

12

When they came out of the saloon, Slocum was jarred. His roan was gone. Dustin's horse was in place, but the roan, which had been tied to the end of the rack, was missing.

Fury surged through his body. His horse, his beloved friend. With a sense of pain, his eyes raked the street. To the east, nothing. But west, about a quarter of mile away, a rider was cantering calmly along on Slocum's horse.

Slocum turned to Dustin. "Some rotten horse thief has got my horse. I'm goin' after him with your sorrel. Just stand by."

He leaped on the saddle of the sorrel, whipped his heels at its flanks, and the horse streaked forward.

Slocum's eyes were on the rider, unaware that he was being followed. Slocum's mind raced: a lowlife, a rustler, who'd steal the false teeth of his grandmother. Anyone who'd steal a man's horse was lower than a snake's belly. But to steal his beloved roan! Slocum was ready to tear the viper to pieces. He gained fast on the rustler, who finally heard the galloping hooves.

The rustler turned and, seeing Slocum racing toward him, panicked and dug his spurs into the roan's flanks.

It was a shock to the roan who, until this moment, had not known the bite of steel on his body. The roan well knew that a stranger, not his master, was riding him. And at this insult, instead of jumping forward, he neighed in outrage, skidded to a stop, climbed on his hind legs, and pawed the air.

The rustler, frustrated, and aware that the rider behind him was coming fast, again hit the horse with his spurs. Bewildered by this further mistreatment, the roan in sudden fury began to twist, heave, and hump. Within seconds the rustler sailed over his head and came down hard on the ground.

It took half a minute for the shock to wear off. He stared, amazed at the roan, cursed vigorously, then looked up to see the big, lean, powerful man swinging off his sorrel and walking toward him.

The rustler got slowly to his feet. "Wait a minute."

Slocum had already seen blood on the flanks of the roan. He swung at the rustler's chin and the man rocketed back, fell flat out, and lay there.

Slocum looked over his horse. There were no other injuries; he looked all right, except that his nostrils were wide and his eyes big with anxiety and anger.

Slocum stared at the rustler. He was a pathetic specimen, bony-faced, scrawny, in a soiled shirt and shabby jeans. A down-and-out drifter who figured maybe he'd make some desperately needed dollars by grabbing and selling a fine-looking horse.

Then Dustin came galloping up on a borrowed horse, dismounted, and looked down at the horse thief, who was sitting up. "We hang horse thieves," Dustin said.

"You hurt my horse," Slocum said through clenched teeth.

The drifter looked at Slocum pitifully. "I'm sorry, mister. I'm dead broke."

Slocum surveyed this pale, bony, miserable man and felt his rage dissipate—partly because of his relief in getting the roan back. "Any man would string you up."

"I know," the drifter said. "I don't care anymore."

Slocum looked at Dustin. The man was down and out and pitiful. "What were you going to do?" Slocum demanded.

"Do? I was hopin' to sell the horse to the Hatfields. He was so great-lookin', I couldn't resist tryin' to take him."

Hatfield. Slocum remembered that the Hatfield gang of rustlers were giving the Larrimore Ranch trouble. The Grady bunch had been hired to cut down the Hatfield rustling.

"Where's this Hatfield bunch hang out?" Slocum asked.

"Hang out?" the drifter stared. "I can't tell you that."

"Seems to me, mister rustler, you got to bargain for your life," said Dustin.

The drifter's pale face looked anguished. Then he said, "They hang out in the high Pine Hills."

Slocum nodded. Knowing the hideout of the Hatfield bunch could be useful. He stared at the man sitting on the ground. "The last thing I'd do, if I were you, is steal a man's horse. It's asking for the rope. This time you were lucky." He threw a couple of dollars at the man.

Then Slocum walked toward the roan.

They were sitting around their camp fire, under a descending sun, sipping coffee, when Dustin said, "Slocum, I'm just ready as I can be for ridin' to Larrimore."

Slocum was watching an eagle soaring toward the massive western canyon. Somewhere on the peaks of that gigantic stretch of ancient rocks the eagle had built its nest. He held the tin cup of coffee to his lips. "Reckon it's time to go. We've lost our surprise punch in Salt Creek. Grady and his boys know by now we're on his trail. That could hurt us."

The low sun highlighted the square angles of Dustin's face, and his blue eyes gleamed. "I'm sick of Grady and his bunch. If I never see them again, it won't give me grief."

Slocum was silent, still watching the way the eagle soared, its great wings outstretched, catching the wind current. It never wasted an ounce of energy in the movement of its great wings.

Personally, Slocum felt they were not going to lose Grady. In the Lawson saloon, he had wanted to wipe Dustin out. Why? Just because Dustin had beat him in poker? Was Grady so mangy that he had to execute anyone who won his money? Well, there were such men; Grady might be one. But there could be another reason. Slocum thought of Bullethead. Had he known anything? He had joined Grady's bunch after Lawson. There had been no time to get anything out of Bullethead; he was in for kill or be killed. If they were ever lucky enough to meet up with WIllie Stone, then Slocum would make it a point to squeeze it out of that dog.

Dustin poured more coffee from the pot into his tin cup. "Lemme ask, Slocum. Don't you yearn to get to the Larrimore? Where you can see Mona again. A beautiful woman."

A picture of Mona, the way he'd seen her at his hotel room, flashed in Slocum's mind. Her beautiful, curving body, her velvet skin, her dark glowing eyes.

"It wouldn't hurt to see Mona," he said. "What surprises me is that Steve Larrimore hasn't put his brand on her."

Dustin looked thoughtful. "Confess it surprises me, too. I figure he's that kind of man. Man with a strong sense of property."

"Maybe. He said the ranch once belonged to your father. Let's see how generous he can be."

Dustin shrugged. "I don't worry about it."

Slocum and Dustin rode west for hours toward the giant sky-reaching canyon, past mesas bulking like giant dominoes, through sage and cedar, through smooth green meadows until they came to a steep rise. It gave a broad view of the Larrimore Ranch.

They reined their horses and looked.

It was a rich, natural panorama, a big white ranch house, smooth rich land, corrals of horses. And grazing cattle as far as the eye could reach. A lazy stream, glittering brightly in the sun, twisted through the land, nourishing the grass and trees, giving it a rich shimmer of bright green.

"That's one nice spread," said Slocum.

Dustin looked impressed. "Funny, but I don't seem to remember much of all this."

"You were a small kid. Small kids see small things."

They rode in, and as they came closer, Slocum spotted Walker in his denim jacket and Levi's, leaning on the corral fence, watching a rider digging in his spurs, trying to tame a rambunctious bronc.

Slocum couldn't help think of the drifter who had torn the flanks of his beloved roan, and again he felt a streak of anger. There were ways to teach a horse without tearing the flesh. Slocum hated to see it.

Walker sighted them, stared, seemed disconcerted, then came off the fence. He adjusted his craggy face to smile widely and put out his hand as they swung off their horses.

"Welcome to the Larrimore. For a time, I was beginnin' to believe you boys weren't comin'."

"Why'd you believe that?" Slocum asked.

"Dunno." His gray eyes squinted at them. "You been gone for a good piece of time."

"There was the bank holdup," Dustin said.

"And you went off with the posse." Walker took a tobacco chew from his shirt pocket and bit off a hunk. "That's the last we heard. So what's happened?"

"The posse rode into a trap," Slocum said. "Ambushed."

Walker looked startled. *"Ambushed?* And Sheriff Trumbull?"

"Dead. The men with him, too."

Walker digested that, then shook his head. He moved back to the fence and leaned against it. "That's bad. Very bad. Never figured Trumbull to be a smart man. A blood-and-guts man, but not smart. There were some good men in that posse. It's a misery." His eyes studied Slocum. "What about the robber bunch?"

"We got one. Bullethead. The others are still ridin' free."

Walker nodded. "Still ridin' free. That's not good either. As for Bullets, good riddance there. He was a tough hombre, did mischief in these parts. Small holdups, but he'd done his share. You boys want to clean up?"

"No hurry," Slocum said, watching the rider working with the bronc.

"I'll put you boys in a comfortable bunkhouse, just the two of you. For the time being. Mr. Larrimore might want to make special arrangements. He's been in Tucson on business. Should be back tonight."

Slocum stroked his chin. "Did you know who was running that holdup bunch?"

Walker looked grim. "Yes. Barnes was here. He told us. You coulda knocked me over with a feather, Slocum. I knew that Grady had a rough bunch, but I never thought he'd try to knock over the Tucson Bank. Just don't know why he tried it."

Slocum looked at Dustin. "Maybe a little birdie told him that they'd gotten a big gold deposit."

Walker nodded. "Yeah, that may be it. Word gets around."

The rider on the bucking bronc was suddenly heaved into the air. He landed on his rump and cursed a blue streak.

"That bronc won't break," said Walker. "Got one of my best men on him. Real ornery."

Dustin gazed at Walker. "Ever think it's not natural for a horse to carry a man? Ain't that what makes him ornery?"

"I know that, Dustin. But a horse is better off working for a man, getting his regular oats, than running on his own."

Dustin grinned. "Ever ask a horse that?"

"Can't understand why Larrimore would hire Grady," Slocum said. "He's an outlaw, wanted for killings and robberies in Texas and Missouri." Slocum had heard that *Walker* had hired Grady, but he deliberately misstated it.

Walker looked puzzled. He stared at Slocum, then at Dustin. Finally he said, "It's me that hired Grady, not Mr. Larrimore. We just couldn't handle Hatfield and his rustlers. Hatfield is one of the slickest rustlers in the territory. Has a big setup for shipping stock north. We've had the regulators trying to hunt him down for the longest spell. On one raid, we lost about two hundred head, then I told Mr. Larrimore there was one way I knew of stopping Hatfield. I knew Jess Grady in Tombstone. He rustled himself in his early days. Told him he could stay on the right side of the law and make money if he'd stop the Hatfield thievery. He was willin'. And in two months, he almost put Hatfield outa business, cut down our losses eighty percent." Walker shrugged. "So you see, sometimes you gotta go outside the law to get a thing done."

Slocum's face was grim. "The fact is that Grady and his boys shot six men in the bank holdup. And they massacred the sheriff and his posse. You can't work two sides of the law. We're goin' to have to do somethin' about Grady."

"Reckon so," Walker said, and his gray eyes looked troubled as he stared into the distance. "Why don't I show you boys your bunkhouse."

After Walker left them at the bunkhouse, he walked slowly back to the corral, his mood somber, his mind busy.

He couldn't help thinking how much Dustin looked like Amos, his father. Sometimes, looking at Dustin, Walker felt a sense of shock, remembering that fateful night when Amos went down. It had been a terrible night, one he would never forget. He couldn't believe the things that had gone on that night, and that he'd been part of it. A nightmare. Poor Amos, a kind, square-shootin' man. Mowed down, brutally. The one saving moment of that night was when Mrs. Larrimore secretly grabbed her boy and the fastest horse and ran for their lives.

When this was discovered there had been hell to pay. The two men who had carelessly let it happen were executed on the spot. His own life had hung by a thread, but he had survived.

All these years, he had thought the past had been buried, but now, with the son come back, alive, strong of limb, maybe wanting to search into the past, it might all be dug up. And Dustin had this powerful ally, Slocum. Yes, it might all be dug up again. And what then?

Walker pulled out his tobacco chew and nervously bit into it. He knew a terrible secret and felt he might suddenly become expendable. And even more, he worried about Millie. Someone had made a move against her—to strike at him. Was it a warning?

When Dustin and Slocum had appeared on the Larrimore Ranch, it seemed to Walker that the fears he'd locked in a corner of his mind had now slipped loose. He could feel the clammy sweat of fear—for both Millie and himself.

He heard a shout. It almost made him jump, but it was the bronc buster, Chet, who'd been dumped again by the ornery horse.

"This animal can't be broke, Mr. Walker," Chet growled.

Walker stared at him, pleased to be pulled back into the ordinary world again, away from his gruesome imaginings.

"Try again, Chet," he said. "Maybe he just needs wearin' down."

Then Walker saw Mona come out of the small white house where she stayed when she came to the Larrimore. She was dressed in a light blue tailored shirt and neat-fitting brown riding pants and boots. She was walking toward a table which the girl had set out for coffee. When she saw Walker, Mona waved at him. He started toward her.

"Won't you join me? Mona said. "Inez, set another place for Mr. Walker."

"They've come," he said, sitting down. "The Larrimore boy and his friend, Slocum."

Her violet eyes looked at him curiously. "They're here? Now?"

"Yes." Walker looked away, his eyes clouded.

"You don't seem pleased," Mona said.

"Oh, I'm pleased."

"Return of the prodigal son. Do you suppose it might change things around here?"

"You never know. Depends on Mr. Larrimore, doesn't it?" He looked at her. "Did you ever think the Larrimore kid would get back here?"

Her dark eyes stared at him. "Didn't think about it, one way or another."

"Well, he finally made it. With his sidekick, Slocum."

She looked thoughtful. "Why shouldn't he have got here, Walker?"

He took his hat off and scratched his head. "I heard tell a couple of bullets were thrown at him."

Mona's eyes gleamed curiously. "I heard that, too. But lots of men get bullets thrown at them, don't they?"

He nodded, lifted his coffee cup, and sipped from it. "They were riding with the posse. After the bank robbers."

She glanced at him. "What happened?"

"Did you know that Grady was running that robbery?"

"Mr. Larrimore told me."

"They ambushed the posse. Got the sheriff and his men."

Her face became solemn, and she stared out at the canyon. "I'm terribly sorry to hear that. A terrible thing."

Walker was studying her. "Somehow Slocum and Dustin managed to keep clear of that ambush."

She nodded slowly. "They were either smart or lucky."

"This Slocum seems to be pretty smart. The one who's lucky is Dustin. To have Slocum near him. A protecting gun."

She looked directly at him, her dark eyes glowing. "Yes, Dustin is lucky."

Walker stared at her. "What do you mean? To get this far? Or because he's got Slocum as a sidekick?"

But she was looking past him. He turned and saw Dustin and Slocum walking toward the corral.

After cleaning and washing up, Dustin and Slocum had come out on the grounds. By now the sun was beginning to set, and hung in the reddened sky like a giant golden orange.

Slocum's green eyes gazed about him, and it refreshed his spirit. He looked at the big white house, two smaller white ones, the bunkhouses, the corrals and herds, the great sweeps of land, richly green, that stretched as far as the eye could see. And as backdrop to all this was the canyon, vast and timeless, its sawtoothed stone painted copper-red by the sun.

"Not bad," Slocum said.

"I had no idea it was this big," Dustin said.

"Lots of money here."

They walked toward the corral, where Chet, out of patience, was staring at the ornery bronc with disgust.

Slocum grinned at the bronc buster. "You've got to talk gently to the horse, partner. Have an understanding. If you jab steel spurs into his sides, he won't listen to you."

Chet glared. "Well, mister, why don't you come and 'have an understanding' with this vicious devil. Get him to listen to you. I'd give a dollar to see that."

"Would you? A dollar? Almost seems worth it."

"I'll give you a dollar just to *try*," Chet snarled.

Slocum smiled. "Never could resist the call of easy money."

Walker grinned as he watched Slocum climb the corral fence and approach the horse. "Well, he doesn't lack nerve. He's goin' to try and ride that wild bronc."

They stood up and came slowly toward the corral to watch what Walker was convinced would be a short, violent, and undignified experience for Slocum.

Slocum looked at the horse, a big-chested black animal with powerful flank muscles and long legs. If he could be tamed, he'd be a fine running horse. He was staring at Slocum with a vicious gleam in his big black eyes. His haunches quivered in rage, and he raised his head in defiance. He'd dump this miserable creature in the dust, just as he'd done all the others.

The horse closely watched the two-legged creature come close, very close. He didn't speak, just looked in his eyes for a long time; then when the man spoke, his voice sounded soft and gentle.

It was strange—none of the others had done this.

But the horse had discovered that all of these two-legged creatures were vicious; they wore iron in their heels to tear his flesh. Why? Because he wouldn't knuckle under.

But if he did that he'd be like his mean-spirited cousins. He'd seen them—docile, tame, all the spirit whipped out of them, slaves to the two-legged creatures. For what? For oats. For what he could find in any meadow. He felt contempt for the soft-hearted ones who surrendered the most precious thing for comfort.

He wanted to run wild, to run for the mare, to kick his heels at the sun, to learn what lay over the next big hill, to see the valley from the highest cliff.

And they wanted to steal this freedom.

And here came a new man with a soft voice and a direct look. As if this one understood what he, as a horse, felt. Did he understand his yearning for freedom, that he did not want the yoke of Man?

The man put his hand gently on his neck and stroked it, talking softly. In spite of himself, the horse felt soothed. The horse searched deep in the eyes of the two-legged creature, and all he saw was warmth, as if the man would be fun to run with.

So when, finally, the man stepped lightly over his back, it did not put the horse into a sudden bucking rage that would only stop until he had thrown the rider or died in the effort.

But still the man was a burden to be challenged.

So the horse began it. He kicked and bucked, but he did it, somehow, with less panic, less fury, less violence.

And he never felt the jerk of reins to gash his mouth or the bite of steel to tear his flanks.

He heard only gentle talk and felt the stroking. He bucked again to dump the man, but the man hung on, and did no vicious hurt.

Then suddenly the horse understood: that a man could be a kind partner, not a hard, cruel master. He could be a companion in the joy of running to new, strange, and beautiful places.

The horse stopped bucking.

Then he ran easy, his powerful legs carrying him straight, as his rider wanted, turning around the corral.

He did it cheerfully.

Somehow, it seemed all right, even natural, to do it.

Slocum eased the horse to the side of the corral, swung off, and stroked him. There was a glow in the big dark eyes.

"Now we're friends, horse," said Slocum with a smile, patting the powerful neck.

Mona and Walker had come to the fence of the corral to watch Slocum working with the horse.

Walker whistled softly. "That Slocum does things real good," he said.

Mona thought of how he made love. "Yes, he has a way about him."

Dustin and Chet came up to Slocum.

"Mister, I don't know what magic you used on this ornery bronc," Chet said. "But you did it. And if I hadn't seen it, I wouldn't have believed it." He reached into his pocket. "Here's the dollar."

"Never mind," Slocum said.

Chet was shaking his head. "Mister, you did a fine breaking job. Didn't think it could be done. Here, take the dollar."

"Keep it. Just remember this, Chet. It's bad to think of *breaking* a horse," Slocum said. "Because if you break the spirit of a horse, you've ruined it. Keep the dollar. Just remember to stay easy when you handle this horse."

He and Dustin walked toward Mona and Walker, who had been listening.

"What's that again about breaking a horse's spirit?" asked Walker with a half-mocking smile.

"Break the spirit of anything," Slocum said, "I reckon you've ruined it."

Walker shook his head. "The world don't run unless you do some breaking."

Slocum laughed as they walked to the table. "Oh, yes. There's plenty out there that needs breaking."

"Like Grady," said Dustin. "There's one that needs it bad."

They sat down at the table, and Walker called to the girl to bring out whiskey and glasses.

13

Steve Larrimore, bulky and square-faced, had finished his business in Tucson with Jones, the cattleman, and was now riding toward his ranch.

The sky overhead darkened with rain clouds, so Larrimore nudged his horse. It was a Morgan with fine bloodlines, a horse that would run its heart out for its rider. Larrimore couldn't help but think about that as the Morgan gracefully quickened its pace. Larrimore felt it fitting that he ride the best. He had acquired a taste for the best when he took over the ranch, after the death of his brother, Amos.

The thought of Amos made Larrimore's jaw tighten and sent a bad feeling through him. But he snuffed it out. Then Dustin came to mind and he frowned. It had been a shock to see Dustin at the dance. Larrimore remembered Dustin as a small fry; he had called him Dusty then. Now, grown to young manhood, Dusty looked so like Amos it was a jolt.

Thinking about Amos unloosened the old feelings in Steve Larrimore.

The dense clouds scurried northeast; they'd hit in minutes, a brief shower. Looking for shelter, Larrimore spotted an overhanging ledge, and he moved the Morgan under it. The rains came down, gray and slanting, pelting the juniper and sage and the ledge over his head.

But Steve Larrimore wasn't seeing the rain, he was remembering growing up with Amos. Amos, the older brother, the favorite son. Amos had been better than Steve in riding, rope-throwing, bronc-busting, all things important to growing lads eager to prove their manhood. But there had been one thing about Amos.

The memories brought Steve Larrimore a familiar flicker of pain. Memories that he had thought buried in the dead past, but which still came alive at a time like this.

Larrimore listened to the rain pattering against the rocks. It was dumb to agonize about the past. He was owner of one of the finest ranches in the Arizona Territory. One of its most powerful men.

Larrimore had discovered in himself a knack for making money. He had learned how to replenish his stock, buy cattle at low prices from small ranchers, and ship at high prices to the Northeast. And he knew how to get fat profits from an army desperate for horses.

But if you owned something good, the coyotes skulked around to devour it. This didn't surprise Steve

Larrimore. He knew human nature. After all, he knew himself—and what he'd done in the past.

So when the Hatfield rustlers became more than a nuisance, he had ordered Walker to get Grady.

Grady was an outlaw and a killer, but he could be useful. Steve Larrimore knew Grady as a man for hire, one who didn't care what the job was, as long as it paid well. There were speical jobs you used a man like Grady for.

Standing under the ledge next to his Morgan, and thinking about how much he'd done with the ranch, he felt a surge of pride.

He looked up at the clouds moving north, driven by a south wind. The sun came out to dry the earth. Now in a better mood, Larrimore rode toward his ranch. He reached it when the sun was low in the sky.

As he approached the corral, he saw the four of them near Mona's house, at the outside table, drinking and talking. Mona and Walker, Slocum and Dustin.

The lines of his face deepened, and his mind worked. He thought about Mona and the way she laughed when Slocum was near. Then he thought about Grady. In town, Barnes had told him that Dustin and Slocum had joined the posse in pursuit of the Grady bunch. How'd they get here this quick? Did it mean they had gunned down Grady? Hard to believe. Grady was a slick devil, with six lives. Larrimore wondered what had happened out there. He swung off the saddle.

Stretch, a bony wrangler, ran over to take the Morgan and walk him to the corral.

Larrimore strolled to the table and sat down, smiling broadly. "Well, it's nice to see you all together." He nodded at Slocum and Mona, but gave his attention to Dustin.

"How does it feel to be back here, Dusty?" He used the name that Dustin's father had used.

"Feels fine, Uncle Steve. Place looks bigger than I remember."

"It is bigger. I did a job on it. We've got more stock than ever, and I built more corrals. We ship to the Northeast market. There's big money in beef, young man."

Dustin's blue eyes glittered, but he said nothing.

Larrimore looked at him closely. "As you know, this place once belonged to your dad. You were a chitling when . . . he died." Larrimore's voice sounded husky. "And when you and your mom disappeared, the place was up for grabs. I did what I could to hold on and build it, as you see."

Dustin nodded. "It's a beautiful spread."

"Well, listen, Dusty. I want you to know that you're part of all this. Whatever you need."

Dustin grinned. "Thanks, Uncle Steve. Mighty generous. Just now, I'm not sure what I aim to do."

"We'll find something for you. I wouldn't mind easing up a bit." He looked over at Mona and put his hand on hers affectionately. "Mona has taken a lot of paperwork off my back."

Slocum looked at Mona, and she smiled.

Larrimore's eyes narrowed a bit, but he went on casually. "And Walker, here, knows how to keep a tight rope on the place." Then he stared at Slocum, at the cool green eyes in the square, strong face. "We owe you plenty, mister. Done a great job helping Dusty from catching hell. The welcome mat is out for you, too. I need all the good guns I can get." He smiled. "We've always got rustlers pilfering our herds. Gotta spill some blood to scare hell outa them."

Slocum lit a cigarillo. "Wasn't Jess Grady doing that job for you? Knocking off the rustlers?"

Larrimore scowled. "Yes, I was forced to use Grady. He knew how to put a twist in Hatfield's tail."

Slocum watched Larrimore, who beamed as he lifted his glass again, like everything now was jake. "Did you know that Grady and his bunch shot six men in town?" Slocum asked.

Larrimore's face grew solemn. "I heard that."

"Also, they ambushed Trumbull and his posse."

Larrimore's brown eyes glittered. He was silent.

Slocum watched him carefully. "Wiped them out. All dead."

Larrimore looked at Walker and slowly shook his head. "That's too bad. Walker, I feared something like that. Grady is a dangerous dog. Unpredictable." He turned to Slocum. "We used him, I told you, to get at the rustlers. Walker figured he'd stick inside the law. But he's hit the bank. That's bad."

"An outlaw does what an outlaw does: robs and kills," Slocum said.

Larrimore shrugged. "The truth is, I'm through using him. He did his job, for which he got plenty. Knocked out most of the Hatfield gang." Larrimore filled his glass and brought it to his lips. "Sometimes, Slocum, one way to fight outlaws is by using outlaws. But you're right, you can't control a bunch like that. They get greedy."

Slocum smiled, but his green eyes were hard. "I wonder if you know, Mr. Larrimore, that it was Jess Grady's best gun, Hardy, who wanted to cut Dustin down. Now that's what I found puzzling. If you're working for a man, it don't seem the right thing to gun down his kin."

Larrimore looked startled, and a flush began in his cheeks. "Hold on there."

Dustin spoke up. "But Slocum, neither Hardy or Grady, at the time this happened, knew I was kin to Larrimore."

Steve Larrimore's face was grim. "You got to believe Jess Grady didn't know. He'd never lift a hand against you, Dusty, if he knew you were kin."

Slocum's smile was deadly. "I'm glad you've got faith in Grady. I wouldn't trust him far as I could throw a horse. He was out to mow us down. I aim to catch up with that gent."

Larrimore shook his head. "Hard to believe that." He glanced at Walker. "What do you think?"

"Grady's probably running like hell toward Tombstone right now."

Larrimore nodded. "That's what I think." He looked anxious to switch the subject and turned to Mona. "All this must be mighty borin' to you. Why don't you show Slocum around. I've got business with Walker. And Dustin, it wouldn't hurt for you to listen." He smiled. "Teach you the cattle business."

Watching Larrimore, Slocum's lips tightened. Then he turned to Mona.

Mona's spirited mare kept up with the roan as they cantered over the smooth grass toward the gray cliffs. Slocum liked the way Mona rode, her head erect and her back arched; he pleasured in the movement of her breasts.

The light of the low sun touched the canyon with pale pink and primrose. For a time they rode a trail that followed the lazy stream, winding south and sparkling under the sun's rays. Slocum saw the corrals of fine-looking horses, then the grazing longhorns. There were cattle herds far as the eye could see.

As they rode, the land near the cliffs became rocky, spotted with sage and juniper. They finally stopped on a patch of grass between a shelter of rocks.

Slocum put down a blanket for them to sit on. "A drink?"

Mona shrugged. "Wouldn't mind a nip."

He pulled a whiskey bottle and two tin cups out of his saddlebag and poured a drink for her and one for himself. He watched her sip. She did it gracefully. Her red hair looked glossy, and her violet eyes shone in the light of the sun.

Slocum thought of the land, broad and rich, a bonanza. "Larrimore sounds like a big-hearted man, doesn't he? Seems to be nice to Dustin."

"Well, he's his uncle."

Slocum looked at the glowing clouds in the west. "Funny, they don't look like kin."

"Kin?" She smiled slightly. "They're not going to look like each other, because they're not *blood* kin."

Slocum frowned "What do you mean?"

Mona shook her head. "Not blood kin. Steve was adopted by David Larrimore as a boy." She gazed at him curiously. "Didn't Dustin tell you this?"

Slocum stared.

Mona looked at him through narrowed eyes and hesitated as if she didn't care to elaborate. But she did. "I see you don't know the story. Steve's mother and father were in a settler wagon train. Got wiped out by Apaches. David Larrimore came in with the rescuing riders. He felt pity for the young kid, bawling at the side of his dead mother. Picked him up, brought him home, raised him alongside his own son, Amos."

Slocum looked thoughtfully at the sawtoothed ridge nearby. "So they're not blood kin. Funny that Dustin never mentioned it."

"It all happened long ago. Maybe it seemed natural to Dustin. Steve Larrimore was always there."

Slocum puffed his cigarillo and watched the smoke drift up in the quiet air. "How did Amos die?"

Mona looked vague. "Don't know, just what I heard. Apache attack. A tomahawk in his skull. Must have been gory. Steve told me just once. Very painful to talk about."

"Where was Steve at the time?"

Mona smiled. "I don't know. All this happened years ago." She looked at him oddly. "Larrimore bother you?"

Slocum looked away. "I just find it strange that a rancher would hire an outlaw like Grady."

"But Larrimore told you why. Grady knows how the rustlers work."

"Why didn't Larrimore use the sheriff?"

"Sheriff Trumbull? Couldn't find his tin star in the morning. He tried the sheriff. Those rustlers are a special breed. Never could find their hideout. And look what happened to Trumbull, chasing the bank robbers."

Slocum shook his head. Trumbull was dumb all right.

Mona looked at him. "It's Grady that gets you, isn't it?"

"He and his bunch have done a lot of killing."

"And what are you going to do about it?"

"Do about it? Let's see. There's Willie Stone, a poisonous coyote. Frank Baker, a clever scout, I've heard, and not a bad hombre. And Jess Grady, that's all that's left." Slocum's smile was grim. "We sorta thinned out the famous bunch."

"And I wouldn't be surprised if Jess Grady didn't have *you* on his mind, too, Slocum."

"I wouldn't either." He looked at her. "You know a lot of what's happening at the Larrimore."

"I work there. Shouldn't I know?"

"You like working for Mr. Larrimore?"

"Wouldn't be there if I didn't."

He gazed at her. "How come Larrimore didn't make a grab for you? Beautiful woman. Smart. Very good in bed."

She smiled. "Oh, do you give references? How do you know he didn't make the grab, as you put it?"

He studied her. "What happened then?"

Mona's smile was noncommittal. "Nothing happened. I live as I please."

"That's nice to hear."

She looked at the sky. It was sunset, the clouds like long stretched cotton tinged splendidly with orange-red.

He wondered about Steve Larrimore. More to him than met the eye.

Mona was looking at him. "Are we going to keep talking about the Larrimores? Or did you have something else in mind?"

He grinned. A luscious woman, a fine setting, an opportunity for pleasure. What in hell was he waiting for?

They kissed. Her lips were warm and clung to his. A long kiss. Afterward she whispered, "Slocum, you do wonderful things to my body."

"Let's see if we can do more." His hands went into her shirt, touching her breasts. He caressed them. Her hands moved toward him, unbuttoning his shirt.

She lights up fast, Slocum thought. The ledge gave them privacy, and they stripped. He gazed with pleasure at her figure, a voluptuous woman, with round firm breasts, erect brown nipples, flat stomach, molded thighs. She was looking at his body with glowing eyes, and, carried by a gust of passion, she leaned against him, her mouth moving in a rage of desire all over him. His senses tingled with pleasure. And he in turn went to her body with his lips as he pleasured in stroking her breasts, buttocks, hips. As her thighs opened, he moved into her, into the moist delight of her. Their bodies locked, their rhythm of movement began, and the pleasure climbed for each; he would reach a peak, then go slow, and he did this again and again until he felt the irresistible surge. Then his body drove with frenzy, and he gritted his teeth at the intensity of his sensations. A groan escaped her lips.

They lay awhile, and Slocum watched the flames in the clouds as the sun moved toward the horizon. It seemed to Slocum that the sky had painted their excitement in colors that they had felt with their senses.

Afterward, she said, "Nothing like making love with a man who knows how to make love."

14

In the living room, Larrimore lit a cigarillo and looked at Dustin and Walker. He felt it more important now to talk to Walker, but he couldn't dump Dustin just yet.

He smoked and said, "I wanted to get this off my chest, Dusty. This is your place, your home. Walker and I are going to work you into the way we run the ranch. If you're anything like your dad, you'll be good at this business."

Dustin wanted to talk about his dad, but Larrimore's eyes looked vague, and he went on talking. "Amos had a good head for the cattle business. Though in those days, I reckon, anyone with plenty of cattle would do all right. Big hunger for beef everywhere in the country, and the beef would come from down here."

He leaned back in his chair. "That's most of what I wanted to say just now to you, Dusty. We'll talk more later. Now I'd like to go over a few things with Walker here."

Dustin went out of the house. He walked toward the corral under a brilliant sunset. Some wranglers were loafing around, talking to each other; some were heading toward the bunkhouse. Dustin leaned on the fence of the corral and absently watched the quiet horses.

Dustin wanted to go over a few things himself, but it didn't seem the right time. Questions about his father. He had to find the right time and place to talk to his uncle. He remembered his uncle years ago, when he was a kid, but he had never seemed to be important. His own father, Amos, was the center of his young life. A strong, affectionate, blue-eyed man who tossed him in the air, making him squeal with delight and terror.

He thought of that terrible night, a dim moon that he saw through his window when he was in his bed, hearing strange cries and gunshots. He remembered his mother coming and whispering for him to be very quiet. They were going for a long ride. And if Dustin didn't stay quiet, bad people would come after them.

His mother took the fast horse, Cyclone, and they rode through the night. He knew something was wrong. Though his mother made no sound, he felt sure she was crying. He wished that he was grown up, so he could pull his gun and destroy what had hurt her. He wondered where his father was, but when he asked, she spoke sharply. "We must be absolutely quiet until we get to where we are going."

That shut him up, though he was torn by fear for his dad. He never saw his father again, and it grieved him for a long time, but he was very young, and the young are resilient.

His mother had grabbed hidden money before she left, and she bought a small piece of land in the southwest corner of the territory, where they lived quietly. Whenever Dustin brought up his father, his mother said simply that he had died suddenly and she had left because of her memories, that she hated the place it happened.

But on her deathbed she had had a strange gleam in her eyes. She told him, "Go to the north, Dustin, to the Larrimore Ranch. Find out what happened to your father. Remember, part of the Larrimore belongs to you. Go up and claim it from your uncle."

It infuriated Dustin that she hadn't told him any of this before. But she felt she'd done the right thing. She had wanted to keep him with her. She hated to lose him.

He buried her and mourned her; then, brooding on what she had said, he started out a week later for the Larrimore.

It surprised him, as he rode north, that an occasional gunman on the trail would take potshots at him. Never nailed down who it was. And when he reached Lawson and played poker with Grady, how close he'd come to Boot Hill. Especially when Jim Hardy, a notorious gunman, invited him to draw. He'd been lucky. His life had been saved by John Slocum, who happened to be there and hated to see a young player get cheated by a crooked gambler.

Dustin watched a horse, suddenly restless, trot around the corral, move close to a mare, and nuzzle her.

Dustin smiled, thinking of how gently Slocum had tamed the wild bronc. He looked on Slocum as an older brother, smart and fast. He had smelled trouble on the trail, otherwise right now they'd be as dead as the ambushed posse. He thought of how Slocum had caught Bullethead trying a trick derringer shot. Dustin had seen it coming and called a warning. Perhaps he helped Slocum a bit. Until then, all help had been coming from Slocum.

Well, Dustin thought, he was moving into manhood now. On the edge of big things. He'd find out about his father.

Then the image of Lucy flashed into his mind. He ached to see her and wondered if maybe he could ride into town with Slocum tomorrow. He thought of her sweet oval face with the merry brown eyes, the female wisdom in their depths. He pictured her pert figure and longed to see her again.

He heard hoofbeats and, looking up, saw Slocum and Mona riding toward him. In the sky behind them was a great sweep of night clouds.

Back in the big white house, after Dustin had left, Larrimore looked at Walker. "Pour some whiskey."

Walker picked up the whiskey bottle and filled two glasses. He watched Larrimore toss off his drink. He looks mean, Walker thought.

Larrimore pulled a cigarillo and lit it. "What do you think of Grady?"

"Pulling that bank stunt? It was damned crazy. But he's a bit crazy."

"Crazy like a fox."

Walker shook his head. "Well, Mr. Larrimore, it was stupid of him to tell Barnes who he was."

Larrimore nodded. "Seems stupid, doesn't it? But didn't seem stupid to Grady at the time. He felt he had figured out how to rob the bank. Maybe he wanted to be famous as the outlaw who cleaned out the bank at Tucson." Larrimore grinned. "Would have made him as famous as Jesse James. That's why he told Barnes his name."

Walker rubbed his chin in admiration. "You understand Grady's mind."

Larrimore poured another drink, "Yes, I understand the criminal mind." He stared hard at .Walker, then quaffed his drink.

Walker paled, thinking of Millie, wondering if Larrimore had been behind that.

"But Grady didn't get away with it. Didn't get the money. And he lost two men," Larrimore said.

"He had Barnes as a hostage, too." Walker couldn't help grin. "Barnes was plenty nervous, I'll tell you."

"Yes, Grady was in a good spot until it suddenly got spoiled. And who did that?"

"What do you mean?"

"Who spoiled it all for Grady?"

Walker looked thoughtful. "Slocum?"

Larrimore nodded and reached for the whiskey, pouring one for himself and one for Walker. "I'm thinking a lot of things are happening now. And that we've got to be careful."

Walker held the glass in his hand but didn't drink.

Larrimore's voice was casual. "What *is* important, Walker, is memories. It's a good thing not to have too good a memory. Especially for things buried long ago and gone. Drink up," he urged.

And Walker, a bit uncertain, drank up.

"That kid," Larrimore said, "has come back here. His mother must have told him something. He's goin' to ask questions. I can see it in his eyes. He's gonna ask about things long dead and buried. Right, Walker?"

"If you say so, Mr. Larrimore."

"Oh, yes, he's gonna ask questions. And he's goin' to get a straight simple story. Remember how we told it years ago. Anything else would be a mistake, a deadly mistake, Walker." He grinned coldly. "How is your memory, by the way?"

Again Walker felt cold fear. He thought of Millie, and he almost shivered. "I remember well how we told it, Mr. Larrimore."

"That's good, Walker. I've always liked you. You see things the right way. And I admire your girl, Millie. A lovely young thing with a bright future. Let's drink up."

They drank again. Larrimore glanced at Walker and shook his head. "You tend to be a bit nervous, Walker. Try and control that."

He was silent, and Walker watched him, feeling sweat on his face. Larrimore would talk when he wanted to, and he expected Walker to sit and wait and listen. He was one sonofabitch, but they had had a fair working relationship for years. But it changed just lately, when a Larrimore scout came in from south Arizona and told him they had buried the widow of Amos Larrimore down in Red River. Then Steve Larrimore changed. He brooded, he became harsh, and Walker would catch him looking at him with hard eyes.

Walker knew what Larrimore was thinking: that he knew too much, and such a man could be dangerous.

"I must admit that I was disappointed in Grady," Larrimore said. "I expected better from him. I didn't expect to see the boy get this far. But they ran into bad luck." Larrimore's face also gleamed with sweat. He wiped at it with his neckerchief. "Bad luck," he repeated. "And you know who the bad luck is, Walker?"

"I'm not sure," Walker said. He, too, was sweating.

"Slocum. That buzzard. He's the bad luck. He's asking the wrong questions. Did you hear him?"

"Yes, I heard him."

"What did you hear, Walker?"

"He said he was surprised that Grady, working for you, was trying to get a bullet in your kin, Dustin. That's what he said, Mr. Larrimore."

Larrimore's eyes were shining from the liquor. "Good, Walker. You're on top of it. You want to stay that way." He puffed at his cigar thoughtfully. "Know what I'm thinking, Walker?"

"No, Mr. Larrimore."

Larrimore laughed. "No, you wouldn't know. But I'm thinkin' that it's a good thing Grady didn't hit the bank right. He's gonna need money, and he'll have to come back to me. He's the one man smart enough to take care of Slocum. He's got five ways to do it. I know Grady. Won't be long before we hear from him. Then we'll act. Things will sort out around here. We'll go back to the peaceful ways like in the old days. Before Dustin Larrimore took up the trail to the Larrimore Ranch."

Walker thought of Dustin Larrimore, a good square kid, who liked Millie, and didn't seem much of a threat to anyone. He looked at Steve Larrimore, husky and strong-faced, a man who seemed to have everything. "Can I ask you a question, Mr. Larrimore?"

"What is it?"

"I never understood what you had against Amos Larrimore."

Steve Larrimore's face froze as suddenly as if it had turned to ice, but his gray eyes glowed with sudden fires. There was a long silence, and Walker felt he had fallen into a snake pit.

Finally Larrimore spoke, his voice rasping. "You'll never understand, Walker, so I'm never going to tell you. Tomorrow night, we'll all have dinner here." He snuffed out his cigar and stood up. "Go talk to Mona. Find out something, for God's sake, Walker."

Jess Grady knew something had happened when he and his boys came back to Durk's Saloon in Salt Creek. It was the new blood scrubbed from the floor in front of the bar. And he didn't see Bullethead, who should have been there. Didn't take much to figure that Bullethead had gone to meet his Maker. And it was plenty clear who had sent him.

"Was it Bullets?" he asked Durk.

Durk, stone-faced, nodded.

"Surprised he'd draw on Slocum," said Frank Baker.

"He didn't draw," Durk said. "Told Slocum he'd have to shoot him in the back. When he thought he had Slocum voodooed, Bullets tried a trick shot with his derringer. Then we saw greased lightning." He mopped his bar. "Not a man I'd mess with."

Grady stared at him. "Durk, you serve the whiskey, I'll figure the angle."

Durk shrugged and went to the other end of the bar.

Willie Stone's grin was devilish. "Looks like we won't have to divvy with Bullets after all. I angled for that. Slocum did us a favor."

"But it's one less gun for us," said Jess.

"Not much of a gun," said Willie. "A thickhead, Bullets, and I never liked it, him stealin' our money."

They were silent and drank. "What's our next move?" Frank Baker said, looking at Grady.

"We go after this sonofabitch Slocum and the kid too," said Willie, glaring at Frank.

"I vote we go to Tombstone and break free of all this," said Frank.

Jess Grady was thinking. "Slocum and the kid are gone to the Larrimore. We don't have to rush. They'll be there."

"We got a rotten haul from the bank, Jess," Willie said.

"I know it."

"We oughta screw more money outa Larrimore," said Willie.

"I'm thinkin' that, Willie."

Willie grinned. "Never thought you were slow, Jess."

They looked at Frank. "I think we got to worry about Slocum."

"That Slocum sticks like a bone in my throat," said Grady.

"You worry too much," said Willie to Frank.

Frank looked at him. "Willie, didn't it strike you strange that Slocum wasn't with the posse when we hit it?"

Willie scowled. "No, it didn't. Why should it? He didn't ride out with them. He was lucky."

"Lucky? Or smart."

Jess looked at Frank. "What d'ya mean?"

"He must have started in town with the posse, Jess. But he pulled away when he read the signs. He read them right. That's what happened."

Willie scowled. "And I think he was draggin' ass with his sidekick, Dustin. And they missed the fireworks. Just dumb luck."

"S'pose he did figure it out, Frank, what then?" Jess spoke quietly.

"Mean's he's cagey. And plenty dangerous. Means that we better worry about him."

"Okay, Frank, we'll worry."

"What I'm sayin', Jess, is if we go toward Larrimore, we go in like the Apache. Quiet."

Willie Stone's lips were twisted in scorn. "Frank, I love you, but you're a pussyfoot. Frank's a scout, Jess. Always likes to pussyfoot. Play the tracking dog. That's jest not my style. We're makin' this Slocum sonofabitch out to be a hotshot Wyatt Earp. He's not that good. I see him as having a coupla lucky shots. But all this doesn't matter. We're not goin' to draw against him. Just watch to get a bullet in his back. No risk. We do him first. After that, the kid, Dustin, will be a pushover."

Frank Baker studied Willie. "He's got to show you his back first."

"We'll find it. Won't be the first time," said Willie grimly.

Grady looked at Frank. And they both laughed.

Then Jess Grady's face became hard and his eyes glittered evilly. "Yes, that Slocum is like a bone in my throat." He picked up his drink and tossed it off. "Let's go."

They stomped out of Durk's Saloon. The saloon keeper watched them. Three dangerous killers. He could tell they were going after the green-eyed Slocum, the stranger with the lightning draw. Durk had seen all sorts of showdowns.

He'd give a lot to see this one.

15

Walker came out of the white house fuming, aware how much he detested and feared Larrimore. If he could only get out of it, he'd take Millie and run for Texas. But Larrimore wouldn't let him get far, not with the secrets he was carrying. Was he to be twisted into Larrimore's destiny forever, just because of something that had happened a dozen years ago?

He saw Mona leaning on the corral fence and went toward her. Larrimore wanted to know what she knew. "How'd it go with Slocum?" he asked.

Mona looked at him stiffly. "Fine."

"Fine. That's nice. I'm asking what in hell did you talk about?"

She looked irritated but answered him. "Slocum? He

wanted to know about Grady. Why he was hired. Why hire an outlaw? That sort of thing."

"I know. He finds it strange, like anyone would." Walker stared at her. "And what else?"

"He asked about Amos. How he died."

Walker's face sobered. "So he asked about Amos. That's how it begins."

"What do you mean?"

"Look at it," Walker said. "These two cowboys come here and are mighty curious. They're not here for a job. Dustin wants to dig up what happened here. Find out things."

She looked thoughtful. "It's natural for a boy, coming back to the place where he lost his father, to ask about it. Why get excited?"

Walker nodded. "You might be right. Mr. Larrimore is goin' off half-cocked."

"Still . . ." She was thinking.

"Still what?"

"He did ask what Steve Larrimore was doing when Amos got killed by the tomahawk."

Walker was silent. What Steve was doing? Why would he ask a question like that? Now that was something to worry about. He pulled out his chew and bit into it. "Slocum has a suspicious mind."

"Suppose he does."

He looked at her. "What d'ya think of this Slocum?"

She thought of the way he made love. "He's a fast gun and he's clever. Hard to know what he's thinking or what he knows. But he's asking questions."

"Like what?" he demanded.

"I told you. Like what kind of a man is Larrimore. Why would he hire an outlaw."

"What do you think?"

Mona frowned with concentration. "I think he's trying to pull it together."

Walker's eyes were fixed on her. "How much do you know, Mona?"

Her voice was a bit mocking. "How much do *you* know, Walker?"

"I know what Larrimore wants me to know."

A small smile curved her lips. "That's playing it safe."

Walker scowled. "He asked me what did you find out."

"That Slocum's a smart cat. He's asking questions. Trying to get at the truth."

Walker's eyes opened wide. "What truth, damn it?"

Mona's smile was hard. "I don't know. I know that Larrimore doesn't want Dustin snooping around. Raising old rocks. Finding out what crawled there." She looked at him curiously. "Wouldn't surprise me if you knew a lot of things. You can be honest with me. Are you with him?"

He thought about it, then said slowly, "I'm with Walker."

"And I'm with Mona."

"Just remember he's got the power. We're walking over a snakepit."

"What are you afraid of, Walker?"

"Remember they tried to grab Millie. That's what I'm afraid of."

"And you think Mr. Larrimore was behind that?" Mona's gaze was curious.

"Yes. It was a warning." He looked at her closely. "You been enjoying yourself with Slocum?"

She flushed. "Have I? I'm glad to hear it."

"Wonder how Larrimore is goin' to like that?"

"He asked me to get close to Slocum. Find out things." Her eyebrows arched. "Well, I did. Got close."

Walker grunted. "I don't think I'd want to be Larrimore just now."

Mona shrugged. "Now? Or ever?"

"I wouldn't want to have his conscience," Walker said slowly.

During the night, Jess Grady made a secret visit to Steve Larrimore.

Next morning Walker told Dustin that Mr. Larrimore had been called away on business and would be back later, and that Dustin and Slocum maybe might want to ride to town.

Dustin was disappointed, hoping to corner Larrimore, but figured that, having waited this long, he could wait a bit longer. And to see Lucy in town was a very nice idea. Slocum didn't mind.

The sun blistered down as they rode the trail in sight of the great canyon, which spread massively to the west, out to defy the destruction of time. The eternal look of the canyon gave Slocum a queer feeling of pleasure. And he admired the stubborn bits of green foliage, the hardy shrubs and brush pushing to survive where it was tough.

They rode into town, tied their horses to the rail outside of Lucy's Cafe, and went in.

Jess Grady often boasted that Willie Stone was the best killing weapon he had.

Jess had recruited a lot of mean hombres into his bunch, and over time, most of them had been gunned down. The one who had lasted best was Willie Stone. What made Willie Stone a survivor was that he was not

big-headed about his draw. He never cared to prove he
was a faster gun than the other guy. To Willie, this was
a small matter. What mattered was having plenty of
money for whiskey, for women, and for good eatin'. He
was never stampeded into pulling his gun to prove
something. If he hated a bastard who fouled him, he had
a way to get even. In his saddlebag he kept a false mustache, and clothes for disguise. Then he'd stalk his prey,
find the chance to get behind his man, and put a bullet
in him. And when the poor slob was writhing in his
death throes, Willie would pass by, sure to let him know
whose hand did the dirty work.

And now Willie Stone was on the trail of Slocum and
Dustin.

Jess Grady told Willie Stone to go to town, hang
around the saloon, and, in his own sleazy style, take
care of Slocum and Dustin. Afterward they'd meet, Jess
told him, at the Larrimore.

So Willie Stone dirtied his face, pasted on his black
false mustache, put on a brown vest in place of his blue
shirt, and a flat black hat that he pulled low on his head.

He stole a horse, and when he rode into Tucson, he'd
bet his last dime nobody would recognize Willie Stone.
He rode through town, looking at horses, and to his
pleasure saw Slocum's roan tied to the rail in front of
Lucy's Cafe.

He drifted toward the saloon, from where he could
keep an eye on the cafe.

After a while he saw the door of the cafe open and
both Dustin and Slocum come out. He knew what he
had to do. Just walk past them, and when he got clear,
he'd shoot and they'd bite the dust, like his victims
always did. Afterward he'd go for his horse, tied down
at the trough nearby.

Two cowboys who'd been drinking, also decided to leave the saloon, and Willie moved behind them, to give the idea they were together. The cowboys were looped and laughed as they walked down Main Street. Willie knew he'd have to walk past Slocum, but that'd be okay. Nobody was goin' to recognize him.

A half hour earlier, Slocum and Dustin had stepped into the cafe, and when Lucy saw Dustin, her fresh young lovely face turned to him with a smile. Dustin's pulse beat fast, and he knew this was the girl for him. He and Slocum sat down at the table, and she came toward them.

They ordered eggs, bacon, biscuits, and coffee, and Lucy sat down to take coffee with them.

"They tell me you might make Larrimore your home," she said to Dustin.

"I'm thinkin' hard 'bout it. Once I get some facts straight."

"What facts?" she asked curiously.

"Well," he smiled. "I'm like a prodigal son come back to his homestead, but not to a father who's alive, but dead."

She nodded gravely.

"My dad, they say, was killed one night, long ago," Dustin brooded. "My mother never knew. I want to find out what happened."

Lucy looked thoughtful. "Millie once told me her father was there the night Amos Larrimore lost his life. Maybe he knew, but never talked about it. Too painful."

Dustin looked at her lovely face and felt the thump of his heart. "Miss Lucy," he said boldly. "Do you believe in love at first sight?"

That jarred her a bit, and she glanced at Slocum, who

was smiling. Then she, too, smiled. "I think you can be hard hit by someone who seems right."

"Well, Miss Lucy, I think I been hard hit—where you are concerned."

She laughed, and looked at him with pleasure. "All I can say is, I'm glad you feel that way."

"Main thing is, do you feel that way?"

She smiled mysteriously. "Why don't you just keep comin' round and find out?"

He cleared his throat. "Count on that, Miss Lucy."

Slocum laughed, looking at them, two fine western specimens. Dustin, brawny and good-looking, Lucy, a well-packed beauty. They would make the kind of strong kids that the West needed so that it could flourish, Slocum thought.

Slocum and Dustin came out of the restaurant and started toward their horses, tied to the rail.

Slocum saw three men coming from the saloon toward them, and he looked at the front two. They seemed lively and drunk. Then Slocum glanced at the dirty drifter behind them, with a thick mustache and a black hat that drooped over his brown eyes. He walked past. Something about the man hit him a bit off. The eyes, Slocum thought. He'd seen them, but in a different face. He scowled, and his instinct for danger made him jerk his head around. The man had his gun out and was firing. It was Slocum's sudden movement that saved him, for the bullet whistled past his ear.

One of the cowboys with Willie turned, outraged by his back-shooting gunplay, and yelled, spoiling Willie's concentration. He turned back to Slocum, whose gun by magic was in his hand, and he was a rolling, moving target, which nettled Willie Stone, never one for accu-

rate shooting. Again he fired, missing, and then he
heard Slocum's gun and felt the terrible wrench of pain
in his right hand, as if all the bones were broke. He
dropped his gun and grunted, grabbing at his bloody,
torn hand. He cursed violently. Slocum came off the dirt
street, watching him. Dustin, nearby, also came up
holding his gun.

Willie again cursed viciously; for the first time, his
masquerade had not worked. Curiously, he thought of
Frank Baker, the way he had sneered at Frank for pus-
syfooting about Slocum. He should have listened to
Frank.

The wranglers turned to Willie, their eyes glittering.
A back-shooter would be hanged in minutes. Willie
Stone figured his time was up, and he didn't intend to
croak under a tree. He began to run, expecting a bullet
in the back to kill him.

He heard the gun behind him bark, but the bullet
didn't kill, just hit his leg, and he stumbled. He thought
of men whose neck he had seen stretched; Willie wanted
no part of that. Painfully, he got to his feet and hobbled
toward his horse. Another shot, and he felt it hit his left
shoulder, pitching him forward. The bastard Slocum
was not goin' to kill him, Willie understood. Goin' to
save him for the rope. He was finished.

He lay on his back in the dust, feeling the hot sun
searing his eyes. He saw a pair of boots standing alongside his head, and looked up. Cool green eyes stared
down at him from the rugged face.

Slocum leaned down and pulled at his mustache. It
resisted, because of the glue, but finally it came away
painfully.

"Well, Willie Stone. Looks like you've come to the
end of your trail."

Willie's face gleamed with fear at the thought of death, which he had given to a lot of men in his day.

"Aiiiie, I hurt, Slocum," he said painfully. "You win. I'm all busted. Finish me off."

"Naw, I ain't going to finish you. I sent someone for the doc to patch you up."

Willie was disbelieving. "Don't kid a dyin' man, Slocum. I'm all busted up. Dead shooting hand, and the rest of me. Finish me."

Slocum leaned down. "Much pain, Willie?"

"Terrible."

"Reckon you'd like to die?"

"I'd like it. Do me this one favor."

"First tell me about Larrimore, Willie. And I'll help you. What's he got against Dustin?"

"I've got pain," Willie said.

"You going to have more, Willie. Going to scream like a banshee. You don't want to go out like that. Tell me, did Larrimore put the Grady bunch on Dustin?"

Willie said nothing.

"You're finished, Willie. Might as well go clean to your Maker. What did Larrimore have against Dustin?"

After a silence, Willie spoke in a low tone. "Don't know. Didn't want Dustin coming back to Larrimore asking questions. Wanted him dead. Reckon he was afraid the kid had a rightful claim to the Larrimore."

"So he hired Grady to get rid of him?"

"That's it."

"How'd you know we'd be here in town?"

"Got it from Grady and Larrimore." He groaned. "I don't want to hang, Slocum. Put a bullet in me."

Slocum looked at him. His lifeblood was dripping away. He looked into the man's eyes. Willie Stone was coming to the end of an evil career.

Slocum picked up Willie's gun and emptied all the bullets but one. Then he looked at Dustin. Then he put the gun in Willie's left hand.

They watched him.

Willie Stone's brown eyes glittered, and he raised the gun toward his head—but suddenly turned it on Slocum, grinning like a fiend. "I'm takin' you, too."

Dustin's gun exploded, and the bullet cracked into Willie's brain. His head hit the ground, the malicious expression of glee fixed on his face in death.

In the Walker ranch house, built one hundred yards from the big white house, Millie and her father had just finished eating. He was sitting silently, his craggy face clouded with thought.

"What is it, Dad?" Millie said. "You don't seem to be yourself?"

Dave Walker bit his lip. His beautiful daughter, Millie, who looked so like his beloved dead wife. He ran his hand through his hair. He was on the edge of making his big decision.

"It's Dustin. Ever since he's come here, it's made this place a stewpot. Mr. Larrimore has gone edgy, I think he's goin' loco."

Millie stared at him. "Why would Dustin do this to Mr. Larrimore, Dad?"

He looked at his daughter. It was time to cure her of innocence. "Because Larrimore, years ago, did some rotten things to Dustin's father. That's why."

"You've hinted this before, Dad. What did happen?"

He looked miserable. "It's just that I'm the only living witness to what happened, Millie."

"What of that?"

"Makes it dangerous for me, now that Dustin is back. Dangerous for you, too."

Her face hardened. "Don't worry 'bout me, Dad. I can take care of myself. You've taught me."

He looked at her with pride and worry. "Larrimore's a man who'd do anything, Millie."

She studied him. "What did happen to Amos?"

His face was pale. "Larrimore paid some men to dress as Apaches. They faked an attack and killed Amos."

"God!" She looked at him. "He's a devil. You knew this."

"Yes. I was a hired hand then. He told me he'd make me foreman, that I'd never again have to worry about money. I was young. Your mother was pregnant. We needed the money."

"Oh, Dad." Her lovely blue eyes gleamed with tears.

"Two of the men who faked Apaches were shot by Amos before he was killed. And then Steve Larrimore set up the other two and shot them. To keep it all quiet."

"Mr. Larrimore is a real devil," she said. "Killed his own brother."

"Amos was the real Larrimore, Steve an orphan boy. But he hated Amos. God knows why. The man's a rattlesnake. Got no loyalty. Do you know, Mona is his secret woman. He told her to do anything to find out what Slocum knows."

She bit her lip. "Mona, Mona." She stared at him. "What are you going to do, Dad?"

"I'm through here. Don't want it anymore. I'm going over to quit. There might be trouble. I want you to get a horse and ride to town, to Lucy's place. I'll join you soon."

Her eyes gleamed with anxiety. "But I want to be here to help you."

"Do as I tell you. I'm going to tell him I'm quitting, collect what's owed me, then come back here. I won't be long."

He walked to the door and looked back at her. "Do as I as tell you. Saddle up and leave."

She watched him walk toward the big white house. Yards away. What should she do? She stood there thinking.

As Walker strode to Larrimore's big white house, his craggy face hardened; he was determined to have it out with Larrimore. He hated to live in fear, with a threat hanging over Millie. He had to write a clean slate.

The corral area was quiet. The cowboys had been sent north for a roundup.

Mr. Larrimore was sitting in the living room at the table, with a drink, studying some papers. Walker looked at him, his powerful body, broad-boned face, his shrewd brown eyes gleaming with curiosity. He glanced at Walker with a cool smile. "Did you talk to Mona?"

"I talked to her."

Larrimore looked at him curiously. He's bothered, he thought, but didn't go into it. "What'd she say?"

"She said Slocum asked questions. Like what you were doing when Amos got killed."

Larrimore smiled. "He wanted to know that? A nosy polecat." He studied Walker. "Perhaps you'd like to know that too."

"Might be interesting."

"I'll tell you, Walker, I was laughing. That's what I was doin'."

Walker shook his head. "Never did understand why you had this hate on your brother."

"He wasn't my brother, Walker. We were a couple of strangers who grew up together." He leaned over to his whiskey bottle and poured two drinks. "Here. Looks like you need this."

Walker took a long haul from his glass. Yes, he needed it. He wasn't going to stay under Larrimore's thumb anymore. Wasn't worth it.

"Something on your mind, Walker? Spit it out."

Walker stared into the brown eyes, then pulled his Colt, put it on the table.

Larrimore was startled and frowned. "What's that for?"

Walker looked grim. "I know you for a long time, Mr. Larrimore. I know what you can do."

"I'm sorry you did that, Walker. What's eatin' you?"

"I've had a bellyful of the Larrimore. I'm ready to move on."

There was a long silence. Larrimore's face went stony, but his eyes shone. He looked through the open window, out at the full moon, then he reached for his whiskey glass and sipped it. "What brought this on, Walker?"

"Ever since Dustin Larrimore has come back, I ain't restin' easy."

Larrimore looked down at the paper on the table. "What's worrying you?"

"Everything. I'm ready to go. You can get yourself a new man."

Larrimore shook his head. "You never had nerve, Dave."

Walker's eyes narrowed. "I have the nerve I need."

"So what now."

"Pay me what you owe me and I'll go."

Larrimore shrugged. "Sorry you feel like this. Well, I pay my debts." He got up, walked over to his desk, and pulled open a drawer.

Walker brooded, wondering if he'd made the right decision.

When he looked up Larrimore had a gun in his hand. "You're not that smart, Walker. Push the gun to the floor."

Walker cursed himself silently and pushed the gun. It fell on the rug.

There was a cold smile on Larrimore's craggy face. "I thought I'd tell you this, Walker. Grady sent Willie Stone into town to take care of Dustin and Slocum. Willie has never yet missed his target. The best back-shooter in the territory. So those two gents are in Boot Hill. It makes life simple."

He smiled malevolently. "It so happens, Walker, you're the only one left who knows what happened the night that Amos Larrimore demised." He paused. "With you gone, nobody will know. Ever think of that, Walker?"

He fired, and the bullet hit Walker's chest. He reeled back in shock, his eyes burning into Larrimore's. He fell to the floor, twisting, and his last thought was of Millie.

The side door opened and Grady and Frank Baker came into the room.

"You did that neatly, Larrimore," Grady said. "Nothing like covering your tracks."

Larrimore looked down at Walker. "I liked the man, but he didn't have nerve. And a man without nerve is dangerous." He smiled at Grady. "You boys might do me the favor to take him out and bury him."

Grady nodded, "Sure, Mr. Larrimore. But we're expecting you to be mighty generous, considering."

"You won't have any complaints, Grady. I just want to be sure that Willie Stone has done his job."

Grady shrugged. "Willie never failed to get his man. He's a one-hundred-percent winner."

"That's good, Jess."

He watched Frank Baker lift Walker, throw him over his shoulder, and follow Grady outside.

He took a deep breath, feeling immense relief, picked up his drink, and finished it.

Then his skin crawled as he heard a voice outside. Slocum's voice.

"Shot someone in the back, Grady?" Slocum's voice said. "I've been looking forward to this meeting."

Larrimore bit his thumb in repressed fury, then, taking his gun, he walked softly to a secret panel built into the living room wall for emergencies such as these. He pushed it open and stepped silently into the space inside. He waited there. It was warm. He felt the sweat begin to form on his forehead.

Thirty minutes earlier, after the shooting of Willie Stone, Slocum and Dustin leaped on their horses and raced toward the Larrimore, stopping short of the ranch. They dismounted and crept quietly to the big white house, sitting clear in the full moon.

They could see the lights through the open window, and crouched behind a big shrub near the house. Horses in the corral silently watched them with big eyes.

"Where's everyone?" Dustin spoke softly.

Slocum put his finger to his lips. "On a roundup," he whispered.

They saw the door open, and Slocum watched Grady

come out with Frank behind him, carrying a body.

Who the hell was it? Slocum wondered. In the glow of the moon, the body looked like Walker. He gritted his teeth.

They were going to their horses when Slocum stepped out, with Dustin alongside.

"Nice of you to turn up here, Grady. Been looking for you a long time."

Grady froze, amazed. Slocum. Alive. This was the last man he expected to see. He managed a smile. "To be honest, Slocum, I didn't expect you to turn up here."

"I understand why, Grady. As for Willie Stone, I'm sorry to say the only things he turned up were his toes."

"Now, that interests me, Slocum," Grady said, glancing at Frank, who hadn't moved. "Jest how did you manage to get Willie? Him being so smart, disguised and all."

"It's not an interesting story, Grady. Instead, I keep thinking of all the men you got killed. A bloody trail. How many would you say?"

Grady smiled pleasantly, turning to Frank Baker. "I don't know, how many would you say, Frank?" It was then he made his move, bringing his gun up with amazing quickness. But Slocum's gun coughed first, and Grady, hit in the chest, was jolted back. He sat down, put his hand to his chest, and brought it away bloody.

Then he looked at Slocum. "I knew from the beginning you'd be a sonofabitch to kill." He smiled. "Always wondered what it was going to be like, Slocum."

"What do you mean?"

"Dyin'," Grady said.

Slocum looked at the red stain on his shirt. "I reckon you'll know soon."

Grady looked at Frank, still holding Walker. Then he looked at Slocum. Then his eyes went empty and he died.

"Where's Larrimore?" Slocum asked Frank, taking his gun.

"Inside."

They set Walker against the corral fence, and Dustin knotted Frank's hands and feet with thongs.

"How'd you get tied up with Grady? You're not a bad one," Slocum asked.

"It's how the dice rolled, Slocum." Frank's voice was calm.

Slocum's green eyes gleamed. "That's too bad. Now just stay quiet."

He and Dustin moved softly to the white house and peered through the open windows.

Slocum could see no one in the rooms. It was puzzling. Slocum walked into the house quietly, Dustin following, their guns drawn.

Slocum found it more puzzling as he moved from room to room to find no trace of Larrimore. In the living room he saw the two glasses, the paper on the table, the blood on the floor where Walker had been shot.

"Nobody's here," said Dustin.

"They said he was in here," said Slocum.

"They were lyin', maybe. To cover up."

"No, they weren't," Slocum said.

"He mighta slipped outside." They walked to the window to peer out.

"No, he's here all right," said Larrimore's voice behind them. "Don't move or I'll shoot you both in the back."

They froze, Slocum wondering where in hell he'd come from.

"Drop your guns."

They dropped them. He came over and picked them up.

"You can turn now."

They turned to see him, grinning, gun in hand, a panel door cut into the side wall still open.

Larrimore's brown eyes glowed with triumph as he looked at them. "Nice little hideaway, hey, Slocum. For moments like this."

"Not bad."

"In war, Slocum, preparation is half the battle."

"Didn't know you were at war with your own nephew, Larrimore."

"I think you knew. Sit down, gents. There's no hurry. Dustin, pour some liquor for us."

He laughed softly to himself as Dustin filled three glasses with whiskey. He raised the glass to his lips and drank half the glass. "I needed that."

He stared at them. "So you got Willie Stone, Grady, and Frank, did you? You're a rough customer, Slocum."

Slocum sipped his drink. "I try my best."

"You even knocked off Jim Hardy, the best gun round here. You're a holy terror, Slocum."

"You're the one, Larrimore. You killed your brother, Amos," Slocum said.

Larrimore stared. "He wasn't my brother. He was a stranger that was raised with me. Like I told Walker before I had the unfortunate duty to get rid of him."

"You killed him, my father?" Dustin's voice was harsh.

Larrimore shrugged. "I didn't kill him. Apaches did."

"That's a lie."

Larrimore laughed. "Well, it's not entirely true. I

hired some cowboys to fake an Apache attack. They raided the ranch, and they did it."

Dustin made a lunge, but Larrimore fired a bullet that hit his shoulder. It stopped Dustin, and he grabbed it.

"There'll be time for you to die, Dustin. Don't rush it." Larrimore's face was hard.

Slocum looked grimly at Larrimore. "What the hell did you have against Amos? The Larrimores took you into their family, raised you, cared for you. An orphan who lost his ma and pa in a raid."

Larrimore's face became stony. "What did I have against Amos? I'm goin' to tell you. Never told a living soul till now." He drew a deep breath. "Amos hated me the moment I came into the family. Hated having to share the love of his ma and his pa with me, a dirty, strange little boy from Ohio. He resented everything I got, everything I did. But Amos was a smart one. He hid his feelings from his parents. Amos was better than me in everything that counted round here. Riding, roping—everything. But I was a better head with figures. Amos wanted above all to get rid of me, and his feelings never changed, even as we grew older."

Larrimore sipped his drink. "When his dad was on his deathbed, and had left the ranch to Amos, thinking Amos would take care of his so-called brother, I knew my time was up on this place that I loved and had lived in most of my life. It was either Amos or me."

Larrimore's brown eyes glowed as he recalled the past and what he had done. He downed the rest of his glass.

He turned to Dustin. "Your mother knew. Somehow she knew. And she feared me. She made her escape with you. I was glad, in a way. I had nothing against her or you. But you would come back here someday. I knew that." He smiled coldly. "As I say, preparation is most of the battle. I had a scout keep an occasional eye on you folks, and when your mother died, and you started to ride up here, I had to take steps. Grady and his boys, especially Jim Hardy, were s'posed to take care of you."

He gritted his teeth with suppressed rage.

"But that didn't happen, Dustin, because you had the miserable luck to run into this hombre, Slocum. It's too bad. Woulda saved me lots of trouble. Because now I have to do it myself." He smiled. "And there's too much involved to make any mistakes. The Larrimore Ranch is my heart and soul. I've gone through a lot of blood to give it up."

He smiled broadly. "Can't tell you how much I cleaned that stuff outa my system, telling you all this. Now it's over for both of you."

He raised his gun.

There was the crack of gunfire, two shots, but they came through the open window.

Larrimore looked at his chest, the blood pumping out red and bright. He turned and stared at the window.

It was Millie, her blue eyes glaring, the gun in her hand. She fired a third time, and Larrimore went down.

She came into the room, holding the gun, her face screwed up with hate. She looked down at Larrimore, still alive, hanging on to life. "My father," she said hoarsely. And again she fired. Larrimore's body jumped. "I could kill him a hundred times," she said.

The light went out of his eyes.

Three days later, Dustin, his shoulder bandaged, and Lucy, Millie, and her beau, Hank Mosely, watched Slocum as he moved toward his roan. Lucy and Millie came over to kiss him.

Dustin shook his hand and looked doleful. "Slocum, I hate for you to leave. But remember, the Larrimore is your home. Come whenever you like."

"I'll remember the Larrimore, Dustin."

Slocum waved his hat, and the roan pranced a bit, as if showing off, then cantered toward the horizon, where a golden sun hung in the sky against the massive canyon.

JAKE LOGAN

___ 0-425-09088-4	THE BLACKMAIL EXPRESS	$2.50
___ 0-425-09111-2	SLOCUM AND THE SILVER RANCH FIGHT	$2.50
___ 0-425-09299-2	SLOCUM AND THE LONG WAGON TRAIN	$2.50
___ 0-425-09567-3	SLOCUM AND THE ARIZONA COWBOYS	$2.75
___ 0-425-09647-5	SIXGUN CEMETERY	$2.75
___ 0-425-09783-8	SLOCUM AND THE WILD STALLION CHASE	$2.75
___ 0-425-10116-9	SLOCUM AND THE LAREDO SHOWDOWN	$2.75
___ 0-425-10419-2	SLOCUM AND THE CHEROKEE MANHUNT	$2.75
___ 0-425-10347-1	SIXGUNS AT SILVERADO	$2.75
___ 0-425-10555-5	SLOCUM AND THE BLOOD RAGE	$2.75
___ 0-425-10635-7	SLOCUM AND THE CRACKER CREEK KILLERS	$2.75
___ 0-425-10701-9	SLOCUM AND THE RED RIVER RENEGADES	$2.75
___ 0-425-10758-2	SLOCUM AND THE GUNFIGHTER'S GREED	$2.75
___ 0-425-10850-3	SIXGUN LAW	$2.75
___ 0-425-10889-9	SLOCUM AND THE ARIZONA KIDNAPPERS	$2.95
___ 0-425-10935-6	SLOCUM AND THE HANGING TREE	$2.95
___ 0-425-10984-4	SLOCUM AND THE ABILENE SWINDLE	$2.95
___ 0-425-11233-0	BLOOD AT THE CROSSING	$2.95
___ 0-425-11056-7	SLOCUM AND THE BUFFALO HUNTERS	$2.95
___ 0-425-11194-6	SLOCUM AND THE PREACHER'S DAUGHTER	$2.95
___ 0-425-11265-9	SLOCUM AND THE GUNFIGHTER'S RETURN	$2.95
___ 0-425-11314-0	THE RAWHIDE BREED (On sale January '89)	$2.95

Please send the titles I've checked above. Mail orders to:

BERKLEY PUBLISHING GROUP
390 Murray Hill Pkwy., Dept. B
East Rutherford, NJ 07073

NAME_____

ADDRESS_____

CITY_____

STATE_____ZIP_____

Please allow 6 weeks for delivery.
Prices are subject to change without notice.

POSTAGE & HANDLING:
$1.00 for one book, $.25 for each
additional. Do not exceed $3.50.

BOOK TOTAL	$_____
SHIPPING & HANDLING	$_____
APPLICABLE SALES TAX (CA, NJ, NY, PA)	$_____
TOTAL AMOUNT DUE	$_____

PAYABLE IN US FUNDS.
(No cash orders accepted.)

SONS OF TEXAS

Book one in the exciting new saga of America's Lone Star state!

TOM EARLY

Texas, 1816. A golden land of opportunity for anyone who dared to stake a claim in its destiny...and its dangers...

Filled with action, adventure, drama and romance, *Sons of Texas* is the magnificent epic story of America in the making...the people, places, and passions that made our country great.

Look for each new book in the series!